Sweet Agony

ANGEL'S HALO
NEXT GEN
BOOK 2

USA Today Bestselling Author

TERRI ANNE BROWNING

Sweet Agony
Angels Halo MC Next Gen
Book 2
Written by Terri Anne Browning
All Rights Reserved ©Terri Anne Browning 2019
Cover Design Sara Eirew Photography
Edited by Lisa Hollett of Silently Correcting Your Grammar
Formatting by M.L. Pahl of IndieVention Designs

ISBN: 9781679445576

10 9 8 7 6 5 4 3 2 1

Sweet Agony

PROLOGUE

Shyly tucking my long, thick hair back behind my ear, I glanced at Theo out of the corner of my eye. The sun had just set, but twilight hadn't turned the sky completely black, casting his profile in shadow as he drove through the busy New York City traffic.

When his mother had offered me a ride, I'd readily accepted, thankful for a way home that didn't include public transportation. I was already so tired from not only my own classes earlier in the day, but two other tutoring jobs before I arrived at the Volkov home to tutor Sofia.

Mrs. Volkov always offered me a ride to my next tutoring client's house or back home, but normally it was one of her security guards who drove me. When I walked down the front steps of their mansion to find Theo leaning against the side of his sleek car, I'd nearly stumbled down to the driveway.

"Careful," he'd called. Moving forward with the speed and grace of a panther, he'd offered me his hand to steady myself. The moment his fingers touched my wrist, I felt an electrical zap to my heart, and it started pounding against my rib cage.

Instead of releasing me, he kept his hand wrapped firmly around mine and walked me to the front passenger side of his car. Opening the door, he assisted me in and bent down. Taking the seat belt in hand, he leaned across me, snapping it into place.

The scent of his cologne hit my senses, and I had to bite my lip to keep from whimpering at how good he smelled. Closing my eyes, I inhaled deeply, wanting to hold a part of him inside me for a moment.

Theo had to know I had the biggest crush on him. Only, it was more than that for me. So, so much more. As soon as I met him, I'd been attracted. There was something about him that drew me to him. Not just his looks but him.

He'd been kind to me over the years, even taking the time to stop and have conversations with me, making me think I mattered to him for a moment. During those occasions, we would laugh together, even flirt, and it made me think he felt something too. The way he would look at me, like he was starving and desperate to memorize every feature on my face…

Yet he never once made a move, which confused the hell out of me. He would teach me a new word in Russian every time, sometimes an entire phrase. His dark eyes would light up with pride and something I couldn't put a name to when I got it correct right away.

He pulled back from fastening my seat belt, his hand grazing my lower stomach, setting my entire body aflame. I couldn't hide a shiver as he winked down at me before straightening and closing the door.

Now, as he drove through the city, I saw him glance my way. I felt my cheeks heat with a mixture of embarrassment at being caught checking him out and need so intense, it gnawed low in my belly. At the next red light, Theo stopped and, reaching over, took my left hand in his right.

Lifting it, he kissed my knuckles, his thumb stroking my flesh and making me shiver yet again.

"So beautiful," he murmured, his voice thick with the same hunger I was feeling. "Let's get you home, krasotka."

Fifteen minutes later, he parked outside my dorm. Before I could get my seat belt off, he was out and around the car, opening the door for me. When he offered his hand, I readily placed mine in his and stepped out.

"Are you allowed visitors?" he asked, keeping my hand tightly ensnared in his.

"It's not a convent, Theo," I told him with a laugh. "Of course I'm allowed to bring people to my dorm."

He pulled his brows together, his entire face turning to stone. "And do you have guests often, krasotka?" he gritted out between clenched teeth. For a moment, I actually wondered if he was jealous.

"So far, I've only had Sofia visit me. And once, your father came up."

His brow instantly smoothed out, and he lifted my hand to his mouth. "Show me your dorm room, Tavia."

ONE

Gathering my books, I placed them neatly into my backpack and grinned at the girl who was quite possibly my best friend—as well as my favorite tutoring client. "Great job on that test last week. I knew you would blow that Trig exam right out of the water."

Sofia Volkov gave me a smug grin, amusement shining out of her clear blue eyes. She was two years younger than me and my complete opposite in most ways, but we did share a few things in common. Like the fact that we were both orphans. Only, Sofia had been adopted by one of the most powerful families in New York from the orphanage back in Russia where she had lived for the first few months of her life.

Me, on the other hand, I'd lived in the same home for children who belonged to the state because their parents didn't want them from the time I was two until I graduated from high school the previous year. There was no family to take me in, no one to adopt me, and no one to care if I made it safely to bed each night. I had been on my own except for the nuns who ran the orphanage and the other kids who lived there.

But I was okay with that. I didn't want to answer to anyone. Didn't like having someone breathing down my neck, asking questions about every little thing I did. And I sure as hell wasn't looking for someone to take care of me.

I could do all of that on my own with no help from anyone. I'd worked my ass off to get good grades so I could win scholarships, first to the most prestigious private academy in the city, and then to the best universities in the state. I'd chosen Columbia because they'd given me the most money, paying for everything, including my books and even the single dorm room where I didn't have to deal with annoying roommates. Being so close to Sofia and my other tutoring clients was a plus. It allowed me to keep working while still going to classes and not having to build up a new client list somewhere else.

The fact that it kept me close to Sofia's older brother, Theo, wasn't even a small bonus.

Of course that was the lie I fed myself every day. And one I intended to continue repeating over and over again.

"Tavia," Victoria Volkov, Sofia's mother, greeted me cheerfully as she walked into the library where we always studied together. I was already standing, and she embraced me, giving me a light kiss on the cheek before stepping back. "How are your classes? Are you eating enough?"

I felt a small pang at having her motherly questions tossed at me. No one had ever cared if I got enough to eat until I'd met Sofia's mother three years before, when I'd started tutoring her. From the first time I'd shown up on their doorstep, looking like a drowned rat because I'd had to run in the pouring rain from the front gate at the bottom of the Volkov estate's long driveway to their gigantic home, Victoria had fussed over me.

Was I eating enough, sleeping enough?

Did I need anything?

I had to stop myself from rolling my eyes the first few times she'd asked, thinking she was just being polite—and maybe even a little condescending. But then I realized she was genuinely concerned for me, and I'd grown to like and appreciate her affection.

"I'm good, Mrs. Volkov. Classes are going smoothly as always. And yes, I promise, I'm getting three meals a day."

"Good. Would you like to stay for dinner?" She tossed her long auburn hair back from her face, her alabaster skin glowing in the overhead light. She was gorgeous, and there were actually two of her since she had an identical twin sister, someone I'd met only a handful of times over the years.

I gave her a regretful smile as I tossed my backpack over one shoulder. "I wish I could, but I have one more stop to make before I can get back to the dorms. Rain check?"

"Of course. Anytime, sweetheart." She put her hands on her daughter's shoulders and gave them a gentle squeeze. Everyone knew Sofia was adopted, but she and her mom had a stronger relationship than some of the biological mother-daughters I'd seen together. "I've already sent your payment through your app. Thank you again for all you've done for our Sofia. I honestly don't know what we would have done if you hadn't helped her so much over the years."

Sofia rolled her eyes at me, making me have to fight a grin. It was true that I'd helped her focus on her studies more, but Sofia was smarter than anyone gave her credit for. She just didn't want to apply herself most of the time. It wasn't that she was lazy, just...bored. And a bored Sofia was a mischievous Sofia. Not that she got into a lot of trouble. She was so carefully guarded and watched twenty-four seven, she couldn't do much that would actually get her into trouble. But there were times when she tried her hardest.

I checked one last time to make sure I had everything I needed and gave them both a wave as I left. Outside, there was a car waiting on me. Ever since that first day, Mrs. Volkov always made sure I had a safe ride home.

As I walked down the stairs, the sun rapidly setting and turning the sky a burnished orange, the driver stepped out and opened the back door for me. It didn't surprise me that it wasn't Theo, but I still felt an acute pang of disappointment that I quickly had to hide when the driver's eyes turned to me.

"Miss Zima," Yerik said quietly as he stood there looking like some carved-from-stone statue. He was my usual driver, but the truth was, I couldn't stand him. Still, I wasn't going to hurt Mrs. Volkov's feelings by turning down her generous offer of a free ride all the way back to my dorm—no matter how uncomfortable the man made me. Plus, I could go over my notes for the upcoming client on the ride.

Once I was seated, Yerik got behind the wheel. I told him the address of where I needed to go as I pulled out my notebook and pen, using the light on my phone to see by.

For the next twenty minutes, my focus was solely on what I needed to cover so my upcoming client could pass his French exam the next day. It wasn't until I closed the notebook that I lifted my head.

Only to realize we were definitely not almost there.

My eyes darted around, unease sitting hard in my gut as I tried to make sense of where Yerik had taken me in so short a time. It was completely dark out now, not even a single shard of orange coloring the sky, and I didn't recognize anything outside the car's window.

There were no streetlights, no passing cars, no buildings. Nothing to give me even a hint of where we were. I felt my hands begin to sweat as I turned my gaze to Yerik, who was now gazing back at me every few seconds in the rearview mirror. Fear tightened my throat, but I quickly swallowed it down and glared at the driver.

"Mrs. Volkov will be upset you didn't take me to my next appointment, Yerik," I gritted out, making sure my voice didn't shake and give away just how scared I was.

From the moment I had set eyes on him, Yerik had made me uneasy. Sofia knew I didn't like him, but she couldn't understand why I never wanted to be left alone with the man. Everyone who worked for her parents would give their lives to protect her, so she couldn't wrap her head around the idea that one of them made me feel like he was thinking of doing very, very bad things to me every time he looked my way. She made me feel it was all in my head, but lately, he had made me more and more uncomfortable.

A hard laugh left Yerik, the sound making me shiver with dread. "I don't answer to her, sweet Tavia," was all he said as he continued to drive.

I hated the way his eyes darkened when he said my name. Hated the way he licked his lips as his gaze dropped from my face to my chest. I crossed my arms, trying to hide my breasts from him, only to hear him laugh again.

Fighting panic, I lifted my phone. My fingers trembled over my contact list, unsure who to call for help. If I texted Sofia and told her what was going on, she would just laugh at me. I loved that girl, but she had no real clue how things were outside the bubble her father had put her in.

I should have already been calling 9-1-1, but there was only one person I truly wanted to save me. The problem was, I wasn't sure if he would even answer if my name popped up on his phone.

Theo had gotten his one taste and, just as quickly, tossed me aside. It was my own fault that I continued to hope he would open his eyes, see that he loved me, and want to be together. Forget the bullshit excuse that I was his sister's best friend or that I was too young—too innocent for his world.

Whatever the hell that meant. If we loved each other, the rest shouldn't matter, damn it.

I tightened my hold on my phone and swiped my thumb over his name. Only to be sent to voice mail after two rings.

Heart breaking a little more even as my growing fear tried to choke me, I forced my numb fingers to dial 9-1-1.

And then Yerik stopped, snatching my phone before the call could connect, and my world was quickly turned upside down.

TWO

Keeping my face impassive, I stood in the warehouse with two of my best men. Ivan and Yury had accompanied me when my pops gave me my own territory. I trusted them with my life, which was saying a hell of a lot because I didn't trust many. Outside of my family, I trusted maybe a handful of people.

The man standing in front of me, two of his own men on either side of him, was definitely not on my list.

My control was already attempting to slip, to show my true feelings for the motherfucker who sneered at me as he waited for me to step forward and start our meeting. It felt like I'd been waiting a lifetime for this moment, to stare into the eyes of the monster who had given the order to have my biological father murdered.

I'd been deprived of the satisfaction of taking out the one who had actually killed Taras Volkov, but I'd be damned if I didn't get to be the one to end the man who had given the order.

Viktor Petrov adjusted his suit jacket, a sign I'd come to learn meant he was growing impatient. I knew everything there was to know about this man, had made it my mission in life to uncover every single secret he wanted buried. I knew everything—from what he had for breakfast every morning, all the way down to what detergent his housekeeper used to wash his clothes. There wasn't anything he did that I didn't know about.

His impatience was what I'd been waiting for. Petrov made mistakes when he was impatient. Which was exactly what I wanted.

"Stay here," I told Ivan and Yury. I felt them tense and knew they wanted to protest, but a single look from me had them both complying as I stepped forward.

Petrov did the same, leaving his two men behind as the two of us met in the middle.

I could have taken out this piece of shit multiple times already if that was what I'd really wanted. From the time I was ten, my aunt Anya had been teaching me how to shoot. With her as my instructor, I never missed. Whether I was a mile or a foot away, I always hit my mark.

But simply pulling a trigger and ending Petrov's existence wasn't enough for me. I wanted him to know why I was the one taking his life. Wanted to see his eyes as the life seeped from his body. I wanted to feel the heat of his blood as it poured from the hole I put in him.

"Thank you, young wolf, for taking the time to meet with me tonight," Petrov said once mere feet were separating us.

"I think I'm the one who should be thanking you, Viktor," I said in a bored voice. "You made it so easy for me to take your stock from you after all."

He clenched his jaw for a moment, before his eyes scrunched at the corners in a full-on grin. "I did, didn't I?"

To get his attention, I'd had my men steal his inventory over the last two months. Everything from guns to drugs, we'd taken it all, leaving him with nothing to sell on the streets. Petrov had been raising hell, trying desperately to find out who was stealing from him.

After the last shipment my men had intercepted, I'd had them leave a message for Petrov to meet me here.

"If all you want is to take over my territory, you could have had your father negotiate." I refused to react to the way he smirked when he said "father." "I'm sure we could have come to a mutual agreement."

"I couldn't care less about your territory, Viktor." I felt my muscles tense when he just grinned. He thought he had the upper hand in this meeting, but that would soon change. I was going to enjoy every second of what was about to come crashing down on this sonofabitch.

"Let's not be enemies, young wolf. In fact, let me give you a token of my great…esteem." Lifting a hand, he signaled one of his men, who lifted his phone to his ear and spoke in Russian to bring in the package.

Every muscle in my body tensed as I heard the door open and then slam closed. Slowly, I turned my head.

Only for the entire world to suddenly feel like it was off its axis.

Yerik, one of my mom's own personal security detail, was walking toward us. He had someone tossed over his massive shoulder. I couldn't tell who it was since there was a hood over their head, but I did know it was female from the shape of her hips and the way she was squirming to get away from him.

Yerik stopped ten feet from me and placed the woman on her knees in front of him. When he pulled the hood off her head, burning rage like I'd never felt before in my life filled my blood.

Tavia.

Her clothes were disheveled, her top torn down the middle, showing everyone the pale-pink bra she was wearing. There was a bruise already forming along her jaw, her plump bottom lip cut and trembling. Yerik, or someone else, had touched her.

With violence.

And I was going to kill that motherfucker.

Her darker-than-espresso eyes darted around quickly, the fear in their depths making my stomach bottom out. I clenched my hands at my sides to keep from reaching for her. If I moved to shield her,

Petrov would take that as a sign of weakness. He would know he'd won, and that would only put my Tavia in even more danger.

When her gaze landed on me, a flash of relief filled her eyes until she noticed I wasn't moving to save her.

I wanted to grab her, hide her away from the evil that pulsed in the world.

From the evil that lived inside me.

"Th-Theo," she pleaded in a shaky voice, tears blinding her. "Help me."

"What the fuck is this?" I demanded of Petrov, turning my gaze back to him. With Herculean effort, I blocked out Tavia's whimper of distress when Yerik grabbed her hair, yanking her back toward him.

From the moment he touched her, he was a dead man. He just didn't know it yet.

"Tavia is my present for you, young wolf," Petrov informed me with a wicked grin. "My token of peace."

"She isn't yours to give," I growled.

She was mine. As she always had been. From the first moment I set eyes on her. That long, thick hair damp from the rain as she sat at the large table in the library of my adoptive parents' house with my sister, teaching her the components of some chemistry compound. I knew the instant I saw her that she was mine.

But she was too young.

I knew I would have to wait. Had known, for her own sake, it would be better if I left her alone completely.

But I was a weak man where Tavia was concerned. I couldn't not make her mine. Only, once I had, things had started blowing up with Petrov, and I didn't want her in the cross hairs if things began to get bloody. So, I'd backed off, promising myself I would make it all up to her once my enemy was no longer a danger to her.

Petrov shouldn't even have known she existed. I'd been careful. Kept my distance. Not let anyone, with the exception of my best friend, Lexa, know what this girl meant to me. Not even Ivan and Yury.

"Oh, but she is," Petrov said in a calm voice as he looked over at Tavia possessively. "As her father, I have every right to give her to anyone I want."

THREE

I was in a nightmare. There was no other way to describe what had happened from the moment I realized Yerik wasn't taking me where I was supposed to go.

Once he'd stopped in the desolate parking lot of some abandoned warehouse on the outskirts of the city, he'd gotten out and come to the back door where I was sitting. Desperately, I'd tried to get out before he could reach me, but the child safety locks were engaged. When the door opened and he came in after me, I'd fought him tooth and nail, trying to get free, but he was stronger. My shirt was no barrier for him, and his laugh still echoed in my ears from when he'd ripped it in half, exposing my bra.

His rough hands had touched my breasts, and I'd lost it, clawing at him. It only earned me a backhand to the face, making my jaw ache from the blow. My pain seemed to turn him on more, and he kissed me. My mouth still throbbed from how forceful he was, and I could taste blood beading where his teeth had cut me.

His phone going off was what saved me. Then he'd tied my hands and put a hood over my head before tossing me over his shoulder like a sack of potatoes. When he put me on my knees in front of a group of men, I thought for sure I was about to be gang-raped. Until I saw Theo.

I nearly sobbed with relief, seeing him standing there. The one person in the world I wanted to save me was right in front of me. His shoulders were tense, the expensive suit he wore molded to his perfect body.

But his eyes were blank, not giving away a single flash of emotion in their dark depths.

This man may look like Theo Volkov, but he wasn't my Theo. The guy I'd given every part of my heart to, willingly handed over my virginity and every other first a girl had to give away to, the one I thought I would love forever… That Theo wasn't standing before me.

This Theo stood there with an aura of danger shrouding him. Everything about him screamed "Don't fuck with me." There was no softness. No love. No empathy. He was ruthless and frightening. It was as if the man I knew didn't even exist, and for some reason, that scared me more than the other man standing only a few feet away.

Then the other guy said something that had my head snapping back.

"As her father, I have every right to give her to anyone I want."

"Father?" I choked on the word, turning my full attention on the man.

I'd never seen this man before in my life. He was leanly built, verging on overly skinny, with a face that reminded me of a wraith. His suit appeared to be just as expensive as Theo's, yet it looked like it hung off him. For a moment, I wondered if he'd lost weight or if the suit wasn't his to begin with. Then I quickly decided I didn't care because this creep just said he was giving me to Theo.

On top of that, he was claiming to be my father.

"I don't have a father," I told him, lifting my chin to glare at him. "I don't have any parents. I'm an orphan."

He looked down at me dispassionately. "I am your father. I have the DNA tests to prove it from when your whore mother showed up at my door, claiming I'd impregnated her. I paid her off and sent her on her way. She died two weeks later, trying to score some blow. I had no use for a little brat, so you were given to the state."

My head suddenly felt as if it was going to explode with all the new information I was getting about myself. I couldn't wrap my mind around it, and right then, I really didn't want to. "DNA or not, you have no right to give me to anyone. I'm a person, not a piece of furniture you can offer as... What did you call it? A 'token of peace'? Yeah, fuck you."

"Tavia," Theo snapped, pulling my focus to him. "Keep your mouth shut."

I shot him a glare but, for some reason, shut my mouth.

"If the wolf doesn't want her, I'll take her, boss," Yerik said, trailing his fingers down my neck until he was cupping my left breast.

I struggled against his touch, shuddering in revulsion when he pinched my nipple through the thin lace of my bra.

A rage-filled bellow echoed off the walls and broken windows of the warehouse. Before I could identify that the feral sound had come from Theo, a shot deafened me and something hot sprayed across my face, neck, and chest.

Yerik's eyes lost focus, and I had only just grasped the fact that he'd been shot in the head when he fell to his knees and then on his face at my feet. I stared, mouth agape in horror, too shocked to even scream as blood pooled around him and quickly soaked into my jeans.

Terrified, I looked straight at Theo, ready to barter anything if he would just get me the hell out of there. He stood, his gun still lifted, and I realized he was the one who'd killed Yerik. There was something lethal in his gaze, savage, and I shivered in fear of him.

It all happened in less than a handful of seconds, and then Theo was turning his gun on the man who claimed to be my father.

"Don't hate me, Tavia," he commanded and pulled the trigger.

Three shots. Three holes in the man I'd only just found out was my family. Blood sprayed across the dirty floor barely inches from me as someone else started shooting. I felt a sharp sting to my side and cried out in agony.

I'd never felt pain so intense in my life as that bullet slicing through me. It knocked the breath out of me, and I saw stars for a few seconds as I had to fight not to pass out.

Theo growled something I couldn't understand as he lifted me into his arms and took off running. I was too lost in the suffering to think about where we were going or who was shooting at us. Theo barked something in Russian that I couldn't keep up with. I wasn't fluent in it like I was in French and Spanish, but he and Sofia had taught me enough that I could follow conversations if I needed to.

I didn't realize we were outside until a raindrop fell on my chest, mixing with Yerik's blood. I looked up at the night sky. The weather had changed rapidly, and now the moon was hardly showing as rain clouds moved in around it, giving the night an eerie glow.

More gunfire echoed behind us, and I yelped in fright when a bullet whizzed by my ear. Theo cursed and shoved me into the back of a car, quickly following me in. Two men were already in the front seat, and one of them hit the gas, causing gravel to spin up as he quickly made our getaway.

The overhead light was turned on, and Theo pulled off his jacket, then his dress shirt. He pressed the expensive material to my side, where blood was gushing like a faucet. "Don't close your eyes," he demanded. "Talk to me."

"What the actual fuck was that?" I yelled at him, then groaned when he put more pressure on the wound. Sweet Jesus, that fucking hurt. "This is a dream, right? I mean, sure, it's a nightmare, but whatever. What is going on, Theo?"

"I'll tell you later. For now, focus on not passing out on me, okay, krasotka?" He lifted the shirt then quickly replaced it. "Fuck. Fuck. Fuck. Drive faster, Yury," he barked.

I felt the car accelerate even more. I wasn't sure if it was from shock or blood loss, but I began to shiver, and I was starting to feel sick and light-headed. "I didn't think being shot would hurt this much," I muttered. A tear fell down my cheek, but I wasn't sure why I was crying.

Because I'd been shot?

Because I'd just seen two men killed right in front of me?

Because I'd just found out I had a father, but he'd turned out to be some monster?

Because the man I loved, whom I hadn't seen in weeks, had just turned my entire existence inside out?

I didn't know, and the world was starting to go dark around the edges, so I really couldn't analyze it much.

"Tavia." Theo's voice held so much authority, and it commanded I look at him.

I blinked my eyes, trying to focus on his perfect, masculine face I'd always been fascinated with. Those deep-set eyes, that perfect Cupid's bow mouth. High cheekbones. Square jaw. The weeks' worth of beard growth was new, but I liked it a lot on him. It made him look older than twenty-one.

"Don't die on me, krasotka. Do you hear me? Don't fucking die." His fingers trembled as he cupped the side of my face with his free hand.

"I'm s-s-s-o c-c-cold, Theo," I told him, fighting the tiredness that was suddenly pressing down on me, praying I didn't vomit from the pain.

"I know, krasotka. I know. I'll get you warm as soon as I can, baby. Just don't leave me."

A sad laugh escaped me as more tears fell. "But you want me to leave you," I mused aloud, and he flinched. "You don't want me."

"Don't say shit you know nothing about, Tavia," he snapped, but his touch was so gentle when he wiped away my tears that more fell. "Just a little longer. We're almost there."

"I really thought you loved me," I whispered as my lashes began to close.

"Tavia!" He shouted my name, but no matter how hard I tried, I couldn't open my eyes for him.

FOUR

THEO

I ran into the ER with Tavia unconscious in my arms, and the medical staff worked quickly. One second, she was right there in front of me, only inches away. The next, they were wheeling her into a trauma bay and I was being told to stay back so they could treat her.

Five minutes later, she was being transported up to surgery. The bullet was still in her gut, but who knew what kind of damage it had done in there.

A nurse escorted me to the OR waiting room, Yury and Ivan following behind, always watching my back. I should have been making phone calls already. To my Pops and uncles. To my connection with the cops. There were at least ten people I needed to speak to, and quickly, but I couldn't concentrate on that. Not when my Tavia was fighting for her life.

Petrov's people were going to be after me now. I'd known that risk when I'd put all this shit in motion. Knew that I would be on some extremely ruthless people's lists for a little while until I took charge of Petrov's assets. He had a brother who would want to step in, who would be after my head.

I knew the kind of vengeance the man would want. It was what I had been seeking when I went after Viktor, so I would be disappointed if his brother didn't want the same thing.

But things were different now. For one, Tavia had been dragged into the middle of this war, and I still couldn't completely comprehend that twist of fate.

My sweet, beautiful, good-down-to-her-soul Tavia was the daughter of one of the vilest monsters ever to walk the earth. It didn't seem possible that the two of them shared DNA. I wanted to deny it, but the look on Viktor's face told me he wasn't playing.

And the motherfucker just stood there while someone touched his daughter.

I tried to keep my cool when Yerik put his hands on Tavia. I tried so fucking hard. But then he'd pinched her nipple, and the memory of how ripe that nipple had tasted in my mouth only weeks before had flooded back, and I'd lost it.

I shot the bastard without thinking, and then I'd done what I'd gone there to do in the first place.

Killed Viktor.

It wasn't the up close and personal death I wanted for him, but there was no way I was going to leave there without taking him out.

His men started shooting as soon as I put the first bullet in him, but it wasn't me they were aiming at. It was Tavia. As I turned to get her, I watched as a bullet pierced her abdomen and the blood began to seep from her, soaking through her shirt.

"Cops are here, boss," Ivan muttered.

I stopped pacing, unsure how long I'd been doing just that or how much time had passed since the nurse had brought us to the waiting room. This late in the evening, only emergency surgeries were taking place, and Tavia's was the only one currently in progress since the OR waiting room was empty. But even if it hadn't been, I would have had Yury and Ivan clear out the place so I didn't have to deal with strangers on top of worrying about the woman

I loved. Turning, I looked at the two men in police uniforms as they stood in the doorway.

They were both about the same height, the blond one maybe an inch shorter than his darker-haired partner, but on the heavier side. His thick waistline made the bulletproof vest he wore under his shirt stand out more. The other guy was probably ten years younger, but he carried himself with more confidence than the blond officer.

"Sir, we're going to need a statement from you," the dark-haired officer said as he stepped forward. "The ER doctor called us, saying he had a woman brought in with a gunshot wound to the abdomen and her hands were tied together."

Fuck, I'd forgotten about her hands in the rush to get her to the hospital. Just thinking of how helpless she'd looked on her knees in front of Yerik made me want to bring him back so I could shoot him in the head all over again.

Pulling my phone from my pocket, I made one of the calls I already should have taken care of. If I had, then these two idiots wouldn't even have shown up. After hearing the voice on the other end of the line, I spoke my name and then handed the phone to the older officer, whose name tag told me he outranked the other guy.

"Sir," the blond officer said, standing up a little straighter when he heard the police commissioner's voice. "Yes, sir. Of course. We will take care of it, sir."

Moments later, he returned my phone to me, apologized for the inconvenience, and assured me I could come down to the station and make a statement when I had time. With a grim nod, I watched them leave.

Once the door shut behind them, I dialed the first person I should have called as soon as I'd handed Tavia over to the doctors downstairs.

"Theo?" Pops said, sounding half asleep.

"I killed Yerik tonight," I told him point-blank. "He was working for Viktor Petrov."

I could practically hear the tension freezing his muscles and jolting him completely awake. Yerik was part of my mom's personal security detail, and there was nothing Pops took more seriously than her and Sofia's safety. Only his best and most trusted men were assigned to the two of them. Finding out one of those men wasn't so trustworthy after all would put him on high alert.

"Where are you?" he demanded, and I heard him moving around. I told him the name of the hospital, and he cursed. "Are you hurt?"

"Not me, Pops. Tavia." My throat clogged with emotion, but I quickly cleared it.

"What the fuck, Theo? Why was Tavia with you?" He blew out a harsh sigh. "I'll be there soon. Stay out of trouble until then."

"Pops." I stopped him before he could hang up. "Don't leave Mom and Sofia there alone. We don't know who we can trust."

"I'm not stupid, son. I'll drop them off at Anya's." With that, he hung up, and I finally dropped down into one of the hard, plastic chairs.

It was over an hour later before the doors opened again. Pops and my uncle Ciro walked into the waiting room, both wearing grim expressions. Pops nodded at Yury and Ivan, who quickly exited the room. Once the doors closed behind my men, I knew it was time to tell them everything.

"Do you have a death wish?" Pops exploded once I'd finished. "You should have told me what you were doing with Petrov. The bastard was putting out feelers. He was talking to Anya, Theo."

I shrugged. "I had heard that as well. But I didn't want to drag you or Tetka into this. It was my problem."

"One that got poor Tavia shot," Pops grumbled. "She's a good girl. You had no right to drag her into your shit, Theo."

"She's Petrov's daughter," I informed him, having omitted that little detail until then.

"Say what now?" Pops's eyes widened, and he took two steps back from me in surprise. "I did a full background check on the girl when she started tutoring Sofia. Anya looked into her as well. Nothing came up about her father being alive—or his being fucking Viktor Petrov."

"His men seemed surprised by the information as well," I told him with a shrug. "And then they were more focused on putting a bullet in her than they were me. Considering I'd just killed their boss, I was surprised they wanted to take her out so desperately."

My uncle made a noise, drawing both Pops's and my attention. "If they were trying to kill her more than they were you, then something is definitely off. Who was her mother?"

I shook my head. "I don't know. I doubt Tavia knows either. Viktor only said the mother showed up at his door after Tavia was born, and he took a DNA test that said he was the father. The mom supposedly died weeks later, scoring blow."

"I'll put out some feelers. See if Desi can find anything." Pops nodded his head, and Ciro walked over to the only window in the room to make the call to his computer expert.

"Tavia could be in danger," Pops said in a quiet voice, glancing at the door as if he expected Petrov's people to storm into the room any second. "We need to deal with this, and quickly. I also need to do a complete overhaul of my men. Do you trust Yury and Ivan?"

"With my life," I told him honestly, and then I quickly amended, "with Mom's and Sofia's lives."

Satisfied with my answer, Pops inclined his head. "I will be borrowing them for the foreseeable future, then."

"Whatever you need, Pops." My gaze wandered to the door as well, but not because I was scared of being ambushed. Tavia had been in surgery for over three hours at that point. With each tick of the clock, my fear that I would never see her again only escalated.

FIVE

Two more hours passed without word about Tavia. Ciro left, but I barely noticed when he muttered he needed to go see about something personally. I was losing my mind, terrified why it was taking the surgeons so long. I paced the width of the waiting room until Pops barked at me to sit, but that didn't last long. I couldn't be still. Could barely fucking breathe.

I needed to know she was okay. Needed to see her. Touch her.

Finally, the door opened, and a nurse came in. She was wearing surgical scrubs and looked disheveled. Her face was tense as she asked if I was there for Tavia Zima.

"How is she?" I demanded, but it came out raspy.

Her lips tilted up in a smile, but it was so grim, my heart felt chilled by it. "She's stable. There was a lot of damage, and as you're currently wearing her blood, I'm sure you know she lost a good bit of it before we even got her open. She's had several units of blood, and we are still pumping it back into her."

"Will she be okay?" Pops asked, and I was thankful because my throat was too choked up to allow words to escape.

She clasped her hands together, seeming to contemplate what she should say for a moment before releasing a tired sigh. "I think you should let the surgeon fill you in on everything else. He won't be much longer now. In the meantime, would you like some coffee? I'm sure the stuff in the nurses' lounge is considerably better than what is in the machine over there."

"We don't need refreshments, thank you," Pops told her.

"Well, the doctor will be out as soon as he can. If you need anything, I'll be on the floor unless we have another emergency." She twisted her lips. "And considering it's a full moon tonight, I'm sure there will be."

Once she was gone, I dropped into the nearest chair, my legs not seeming to want to support me any longer. Tavia was stable, but that didn't tell me anything else other than she was alive. I was thankful for that much, at least, but it was everything the nurse had left unspoken that was making me weak-kneed.

Leaning forward, I put my elbows on my knees and thrust my fingers into my hair, pulling at the roots. She had to be okay. If nothing else, the past five weeks without her had proven to me that I couldn't live without her. I'd been miserable, missing her so fucking much, it was like I'd had a part of myself amputated. Only, I didn't know which part, so I was constantly living with a ghost appendage. An achy, empty spot somewhere in my body that would never be the same again.

A cup of something hot was suddenly shoved into my hand, and I lifted my head to look at Pops. "It helps," he told me, nodding at the cup. "Drink it."

Cautiously, I took a sip of the coffee he'd produced. It was black and smelled weak, but when I took a swallow, it was sickeningly sweet. Forcing myself to swallow what was in my mouth, I set the cup on the floor beside my feet.

"When your mom had her kidney transplant, I was a nervous wreck," Pops said as he took the seat to my left.

"I remember."

When I was a kid, Mom's diabetes had fucked up her kidneys. Thankfully, her twin sister had been ready, willing, and able to give her one of her own kidneys. I remembered how stressed Pops was the day of the surgery. I'd never seen him cry before, but when the doctors finally came to tell us she was out of surgery and doing well, he'd broken down. Unashamedly, he'd cried in front of everyone, thankful she was okay.

"How long have you loved Tavia?" he surprised me by asking.

"From the moment I set eyes on her," I told him honestly, and I felt him tense. "I didn't touch her back then, though. She was too young. But about a month or so ago, I drove her home for Mom."

And I'd been weak. I couldn't keep my hands off her.

All Pops did was nod, and we both stayed quiet for a while. Thirty minutes passed before the doctor came to speak to us. His scrubs and the surgical cap on his head were drenched with sweat, and he looked even grimmer than the nurse had earlier. The look on his face had the oxygen in my lungs turning to ice, making it hard to breathe as he approached.

I started to stand, but he shook his head, motioning for Pops and me to stay seated, and he took the chair directly in front of us. "I need a breather, gentlemen, so let's do this sitting." He pulled off his cap and ran his fingers over his short, graying hair, but then his eyes focused directly on me. "Are you Tavia's boyfriend?"

"She's mine," I confirmed.

"So, you were aware she was pregnant, then?"

"What?" Every muscle in my body seized, my heart contracting. "No, I had no idea she… Wait. Was?" The past tense hit me hard.

"I'm sorry to say she miscarried."

Swallowing down the lump choking me, I stored that away for the moment. I couldn't focus on the loss suddenly pressing down on me. "How is Tavia?" I asked.

He sat back in his chair. "Gut wounds can be tricky, but as long as she takes it easy and has good

aftercare, she should make a full recovery—
provided she doesn't get an infection."

My relief was so strong, I felt dizzy for a
second and had to blink to focus on the doctor. "Can
I see her?" I didn't care that I sounded desperate.
That was exactly what I was right then.

"She's in recovery right now, but once she's
moved into a room, you can see her all you want...
As long as she permits it." He stood. "She might not
have known she was pregnant. This miscarriage may
come as a complete surprise to her. Nonetheless, we
should handle telling her delicately."

I nodded my agreement. He shook my hand and
then Pops's, telling us someone would let us know
once Tavia was comfortably in a room. Pops
followed him out the door, already making
arrangements to make sure Tavia had a private room
and any other luxury the hospital could offer.

As the door closed behind them, I fell back
against my chair, the reality of what the doctor said
hitting me full force. Pregnant. Tavia had been
carrying my baby. I wanted to think she didn't know,
but what if she had? What if those times she'd called
and I hadn't answered she was trying to tell me she
was going to have my child?

Fuck.

I'd completely messed up with her. She probably thought she had to go through the pregnancy alone. Had to raise our baby alone.

All her life, she had felt just that. Alone. No one to take care of her. No one to worry for her. No one to love her.

I'd make sure she never felt like that again, I vowed silently. I wasn't ever going to let her down again.

Reality came back to me slowly. The scraping of a chair across the floor filled my ears, then a chilled hand touching mine, the deep inhale of someone before their lips brushed over my knuckles.

Then the pain hit me, and I moaned pitifully before blinking my eyes open. The lighting in the room was dim, but there was daylight shining through the partially shut blinds. The smell of antiseptic was suddenly harsh to my senses, and I turned my head as I vomited, but there was nothing but gastric juices able to come up.

The contraction of my muscles as I heaved only made the pain that much more intense, and I was sobbing by the time my stomach calmed down.

"It's okay," a deep voice assured me, a heavy hand stroking soothingly over my back.

Disbelief at who it was had me lifting my head to make sure I wasn't hearing things. But no, Theo was actually there, his face gray and set in hard lines as he lifted a damp washcloth and wiped it over my brow and then my mouth.

Tossing away the cloth, he took two tissues from a box and mopped up my tears. "Better?"

All I could do was nod, too stunned he was there, taking care of me. Being kind.

Cupping the back of my head, he eased me onto my back and then tucked the covers around me before taking the chair directly beside the bed.

"Are you in a lot of pain?" His voice was so gentle, full of the same tenderness he'd used when he was deep inside me all those weeks ago. Only now, I knew better. He got what he wanted, and then I'd meant nothing to him.

I nodded again, refusing to speak to him.

He drew his brows together, but he hit the call button tied to my bed rail. Not even ten seconds later, the door opened, and not one but two nurses walked in after a brisk knock.

Theo didn't take his eyes off me as he instructed them to give me something to better manage my pain.

"Of course, Mr. Volkov," the more petite of the two said. "We can hook her up to a morphine pump, and she can dispense as much or a little pain medication as she feels she needs."

The second nurse stepped out and was back quickly, pushing some kind of machine that looked like the one holding my IV and the bag of blood that was now empty. Within minutes, the thing was hooked up to my IV site, and the two nurses instructed me how much would be dispensed per hour. Once they were done, they asked if I needed anything else, but I only shook my head, and they left.

Theo once again took his seat, but I focused on the little red button I was supposed to push to administer the morphine.

"Tavia..." I pressed the button once, but that didn't even faze my pain level. "You haven't said anything yet." I pushed the button again and then twice more before the pain began to fade. Only then, the world began to spin, and I quickly closed my eyes before I became nauseated again. "Baby, talk to me."

I turned my head away from him without opening my eyes. I knew it was childish to give him the silent treatment, but my heart was too broken to care. All I wanted was for him to leave me alone, something I knew he was good at. The morning after I'd given in to my feelings for this man and he'd taken my virginity, I'd woken up to an empty bed, and I hadn't seen him again until...

Until Yerik took off that hood, and I saw Theo standing there looking like the ruthless mobster he apparently was.

I heard Theo exhale heavily. "Okay, krasotka. Rest. We will talk later."

I hit the button one more time and drifted off to sleep, wanting away from him just as much as I wanted away from the pain.

I wasn't sure how long I slept, but the next time I became aware of my surroundings, it was to fierce whispering. "We have to get her away from here," a quiet female voice was saying, and I lifted my lashes to see who it was.

The lighting was even dimmer than it had been earlier, and I quickly realized that was because it was dark outside now. Theo stood by the window, his father on one side of him and a woman with dark hair I vaguely remembered as his aunt on the other.

"If she goes, I go," Theo told her, a determined look I knew well on his face. "I'm not leaving her alone. Not now."

His father muttered something savage in Russian I didn't understand before finally blowing out a harsh exhale and nodding. "Okay. And just where do you plan on taking her?"

"You know where I'm taking her," Theo told him with a neutral expression, his thickly muscled arms crossed over his chest.

"It makes sense," his aunt said, tilting her head to the side. "Few people know our connection to them. Ciro made sure of that. Other than using them for protection for certain cargo hauls, we don't often have business with them. And those are some scary motherfuckers. Petrov would think twice before stepping into their territory."

"It's decided, then. And we do not tell your mom and sister about any of this." Adrian Volkov looked hard at the two of them. "I mean it, Anya. Not a single detail is to be shared with either Victoria or Sofia."

"I heard you," she told him with a roll of her eyes. "But I will have to tell Cristiano. There's no getting past that."

"Just make sure he knows not to discuss it with my wife, and I don't care." He put a hand on Theo's shoulders. "We have your back, son. Remember that. Tavia is like family to us."

Theo nodded grimly, and Adrian stepped back, dropping his hands to his sides. "I'll make the arrangements to have her transported to the airport. Anya, have one of the Vitucci jets ready for takeoff within the hour."

"Already on it," she assured him. I watched through my lashes as she hugged Theo, heard the faint whisper as she spoke something into his ear and stepped back. "I'm only a phone call away. No matter the time, no matter what I'm doing, I will drop everything for you. Stay safe. Watch your back. And trust no one but the Hannigans."

"I know, Tetka."

"And try to steer any trouble away from Nova, or Ryan will be pissed." She grinned and patted him on the jaw. "I would hate for my son to kill my favorite nephew."

Theo grinned for a second, but it quickly dropped. "I will ensure Nova's safety. It's not my plan to put any of them at risk, Tetka. Not Nova or Lexa or anyone else. I only want to keep Tavia safe."

"I know, and I trust your judgment." She turned to go. "And by the way, your girl is awake. Has been for the last few minutes. You might want to start explaining before she freaks out."

I stiffened, my eyes snapping open wide. I hadn't made a sound since I'd woken up, and she hadn't even glanced my way. How could she possibly know I was awake?

I was still trying to figure that out as the door closed behind her and Theo crossed to sit beside my bed once again. "We have to talk, krasotka," he said in that tender voice I'd always loved.

"What's going on? I don't understand anything, Theo."

Sighing heavily, he lifted my hand and kissed my palm. Warmth flooded up my arm, going straight to my heart and then spreading outward. "A lot of things have come to light while you were sleeping. I know it must have been a shock to learn that Viktor Petrov was your father. I'm sure his men were just as floored to learn the news. But they must have also known who your mother was, because they were aiming directly for you. Which is why we have to get you out of here as quickly and as quietly as possible."

My head was starting to ache from everything he was throwing at me, and I didn't understand a word of it. "What does my mother have to do with any of this? I don't even know who she was."

"In my world, everyone has enemies, Tavia. Everyone. Viktor had more than most, me included. But there is one family in particular that Petrov and his brother have always vowed to destroy down to the last drop of blood. No one had thought much of the feud between Petrov and Bykov because as far as anyone knew, there was no one left in the Bykov line. My uncle did some digging and found out that your birth mother was Irena Bykov." He paused as if waiting for that to sink in, but the drugs still must have been going strong because my head felt foggy.

I lay there just looking at him, not sure what he expected me to do. None of those names meant anything to me. So what that Irena Bykov was my mother? She was dead, and I didn't even remember the woman. She was a faceless shadow to me.

"Tavia, Viktor's brother wants you dead." Theo's handsome, masculine face tensed even more as he spoke those words, making my stomach knot. "For no other reason than who your mother was. Everyone thought there was no more Bykov blood left, but now it seems there is. You. Why Viktor let you live when he first found out about your existence is anyone's guess, but his brother, Adas Petrov, won't be so generous. We have to get you away from here until the bastard has been dealt with."

"Okay," I whispered, feeling weak and helpless and in complete agony from the pain in my abdomen. What choice did I really have anyway? It seemed like Theo was totally in charge of everything, including my life.

Someone wanted to kill me, and I couldn't trust anyone, not even the man sitting beside me. Yet, I had no one else to help me. No one else who cared if I lived or died.

At least, with Theo, I might stand a slight chance.

SEVEN

By dawn, we were in the air on one of my aunt's private jets, headed for California. My friend Lexa knew I was coming, as did her parents. Staying with them, surrounding Tavia with the Angel's Halo MC to protect her, was the only option I really had at that point.

I didn't know who in Pops's security was tainted, and I wasn't going to put Tavia at risk by chancing it. With the MC, I knew who I could trust— the Hannigans, and by default, the Reids. On top of that, Lexa had just married the local sheriff, and I knew I could trust him most of all.

I wouldn't say Ben Davis and I were best buds or anything, but the guy tolerated me more now than he had at our first meeting. That Lexa was now his wife made it slightly easier for him to accept that she was one of my—possibly my only—real friends.

Tavia slept most of the flight, only waking up once when we hit some turbulence. And she quickly fell back to sleep once I'd administered one of the shots into her IV line filled with the pain medication the hospital had supplied for our trip.

Five men in MC cuts were waiting for us at the airport, along with an SUV to transport us to Creswell Springs. Out here, they were their own law. They only answered to my family when they were doing a protection run for us, and I knew better than to assume I had any authority over them. It was Lexa's mom, Raven, who sat behind the wheel of the blacked-out vehicle, her sister-in-law Felicity Hannigan in the passenger seat beside her. Felicity was my true connection to the MC as she was my uncle Ciro's cousin, something only a few people in the world knew, and that was exactly how it would stay.

Once I'd carried Tavia off the plane and carefully placed her in the back seat, the MC escorted us to Raven's house. She and her husband lived in her childhood home with her eldest brother

Jet and Felicity. The house was huge, and at one time, all of the Hannigan siblings had lived under the same roof with their significant others. Now they were spread out around the small town, each of them having had their own children.

Tavia didn't stir on the drive to their house, and she barely lifted her lashes when the SUV stopped in the driveway. Carefully, I shifted her head off me and got out before reaching back in and lifting her into my arms.

Raven and Felicity showed us upstairs to a guest room. As I laid Tavia in the middle of the bed, she moaned pitifully and looked up at me. "Where are we?" she asked in a voice weak with pain and confusion.

"We made it to the safe house, krasotka," I murmured, brushing my lips over her brow.

"Theo, I need to check her incisions," Raven reminded me in a stern yet tender voice, so as not to frighten Tavia.

Reluctantly, I stepped out of the way. For the first time, Tavia saw Raven and frowned. "Who are you?"

Lexa's mom was a tall, willowy blonde with very short hair. It had started growing back after her chemotherapy treatments had stopped. She was thankfully cancer-free now, but the chemo had made her pretty sick. Once she had started to lose her hair from the treatments, she had shaved her head. And surprisingly, her sisters-in-law had as well, to show their support.

Raven had always intimidated me, almost as much as my aunt Anya did. Raven seemed like a force of nature. Lexa joked more than once that her mom was the one who ran the MC, and her father, who was the MC president, simply sat back and let her. It wasn't completely true, but there was some validity to it. Something I'd seen up close and personally on a few occasions.

Raven's mouth tilted up in a half smile, but her green eyes were full of kindness, something that was fairly rare from the MC queen unless she was dealing with Lexa or Nova. "My name is Raven Hannigan Reid, Tavia. I guess you can say I'm your nurse. I'll be taking care of you until you're back on your feet. Is it okay if I look at the incisions on your abdomen? I need to make sure nothing is inflamed or oozing at this point."

Tavia looked to me for confirmation, and I nodded. "Sure?"

Laughing softly, Raven glanced at me. "Maybe Theo would be kind enough to bring up the breakfast tray Flick is working on for you."

I got the hint and started for the door, only to pause with my hand on the doorknob. "Mrs. Reid..."

"It's okay, Theo. I know about everything. Doc and I had a very informative conversation with her surgeon earlier."

Nodding, I opened the door, but I looked at Tavia before walking through it. "I will be right back. You can trust her, krasotka. No one in this house will harm you. I promise."

Outside her closed bedroom door, I shut my eyes, leaning my forehead against the thick wood. Exhaustion was pressing down on me hard, but I couldn't sleep until I knew Tavia was comfortable — and safe. There had been no time to tell her about the miscarriage, but I knew I needed too soon.

After she was settled, I vowed. Then I would tell her everything.

Downstairs, Felicity was working on the tray. Tavia was on a liquid diet for a few days, so Felicity was heating up some homemade chicken broth. She lifted her head when I entered the kitchen, a gentle smile tilting her lips. Her hair was just as short as her sister-in-law's, only instead of the light shade of blond Raven's was, Felicity's was a pretty chestnut color. Her blue eyes reminded me of my uncle's, only where his were guarded and deadly, hers were almost always soft and full of tenderness.

"I'm nearly done with her tray, sweetheart." She placed a bowl on the tray and then a spoon wrapped in a paper towel. "Don't worry about a thing where your Tavia is concerned. Raven has taken care of plenty of brothers who had a gunshot to the gut. She's a pro at this point."

"I trust her—and you," I assured her. "That's not what I'm worried about. I...I really don't know how to break it to her that she had a miscarriage."

Felicity paused in the act of pouring the broth into the bowl. "Be gentle with her. Be supportive. Let her cry as much as she wants. Let her scream if that helps. No matter how you tell her, it's going to come as a huge surprise, and it will break her heart. Preparing for something like that just isn't possible. But supporting her after you tell her, that's the important part."

I took her advice and stored that for later. Once the tray was ready, I took it upstairs. By the time I returned to Tavia's room, Raven had her tucked in, and she seemed more relaxed.

Looking down at her, I realized how small she seemed. How fragile. Her face was pale, making the slight sprinkle of freckles across her nose and cheeks stand out more. She was the ghost of the girl I'd spent the past three years secretly loving.

"Hungry?" I asked as I placed the tray across her lap and sat on the edge of the bed.

"Not really," she said with a grimace at the broth.

"It might not look appealing," Raven said with a small smile. "But it will give your body the energy it needs to heal. Try a little of it for now. In a few days, we can move you up to softer foods if you can tolerate the fluids."

Gathering her supplies, Raven straightened up the side table where she had placed everything Tavia would need. "Let me know if your pain becomes too much. I can give you something for it."

Tavia groaned. "I'm getting tired of all the pain meds. They make me sick to my stomach, and I'm cramping so bad right now. Could all of this trigger my period?"

Raven looked at me, and I held my breath, knowing it was time to explain about the baby. "I'll be downstairs if you need me," she said softly as she left.

I watched her until the door closed quietly behind her, before looking back at Tavia. She was staring disgustedly at the bowl of broth, so I moved the tray to the side table and took her hands in mine.

"Tavia, I need to tell you something."

She scrunched up her brow. "More bad news?"

I sat there just looking at her for a long moment, trying to find the words to tell her our baby was gone. Her question to Raven told me she hadn't known she was pregnant, and I didn't know if that was a relief for me or not. If she hadn't known, then she hadn't been trying to tell me when I'd been avoiding her calls.

"Your cramping isn't from your period," I told her.

"And you're such an expert on period cramps?" She laughed slightly, only to groan in pain. "Damn, even that makes me hurt."

"Tavia, baby…" I closed my eyes and prayed for strength before finally just blurting it out. "You were pregnant. During surgery, you had a miscarriage."

What little color was still in her face drained from her. "I-I'm going to be sick," she whispered.

I grabbed the small bowl sitting on the nightstand holding fresh bandages and other first aid items. After emptying it, I pushed it close to Tavia's face just as she started to vomit.

The contracting of her stomach muscles made her cry, but I wasn't sure if it was the pain or the loss of the baby that had her sobbing by the time she was done.

Weakly, she fell back against the pillows and then curled into a ball. "Go away, Theo," she cried. "Please, just...go away."

"I'm not leaving you," I gritted out, rubbing her back as she turned onto her side.

"Why not?" she demanded, her voice full of hurt and anger. "You're so good at it. All you ever do is leave me."

"Baby—"

"Just stop it, Theo!" she yelled. "Stop pretending you care. We both know you don't, so just leave me the hell alone."

"You don't know anything," I told her softly, refusing to raise my voice. She was hurting and needed to take her emotional pain out on someone. If it made her feel better, I would let her yell whatever she wanted at me. Fuck, I'd sit still and let her beat the hell out of me if that would make her feel better. But I refused to let her think I didn't care about her. "I only backed away because I didn't want you to get hurt while I was dealing with Viktor. He could have used you against me, and I didn't want to pull you into the war I was starting."

"Great job there, Mr. Noble." She scrubbed at the tears flooding down her face. "Did you know I was his daughter before you fucked me? Was that part of the plan? Did you think that would piss him off too?"

"I found out he was your father at the same time you did. I thought I knew everything there was to know about Viktor Petrov, but you were his best-kept secret."

She snorted indelicately. "Apparently." When I continued to rub her back, she slapped my hand away. "Don't touch me. Don't talk to me. Don't even look at me. I hate you, Theo."

"Hate me, then," I told her. "But I'll always love you, krasotka."

"Yeah, okay." Angrily, she sat up, her face pinched in pain as she glared at me. "I'm done listening to your lies and your bullshit. I'm stuck in this bed for the moment, helpless and reliant on you and the people who live here. Right now, I'll take the strangers over you. Fuck, I'd take the devil himself over you at this point."

EIGHT

I held back my sobs until the door closed behind Theo. But as soon as I heard the soft click, telling me he was on the other side and I no longer had those dark eyes on me, I couldn't hold on any longer.

My anger at him, at myself, at the fucking world, rolled into the deep, agonizing feeling of loss I'd felt from the moment Theo told me I'd had a miscarriage. Despite not trusting him, for some reason, I believed him when he told me I'd lost the baby while in surgery.

The baby.

I covered my lower stomach with my hands, and two fat tears fell over my lashes. I hadn't even realized there was a baby.

How could I not know?

Wasn't a woman inherently supposed to know these things about herself when she had a new life growing inside her? Only I hadn't. Between school and working with my other tutoring clients, I had been so damn busy. Something I'd been thankful for because it had helped take my mind off the fact that Theo had dropped me as soon as he'd gotten what he wanted.

Theo.

Theo's baby.

Like its father, my precious little nugget obviously hadn't wanted me any more than Theo did. But I would have wanted him or her. I would have loved that baby so much, and it would have loved me too.

Another sob shook my shoulders, making my body throb in agony from the way my stomach tensed and clenched over and over again.

What would that have felt like, being loved by someone? I'd never experienced that from anyone; not a single person in my life had ever loved me. I'd been tossed aside practically from infancy, discarded like yesterday's trash and left to fend for myself. I mattered to zero people, and I'd thought I was okay with that.

But now, knowing that there had been the possibility of someone caring for me, if only just a little, made it impossible to breathe for the agony of the loss I was feeling. It hurt worse than the pain in my abdomen. It hurt worse than any pain I'd ever felt in my entire life.

It was enough to make me hate the world as a whole. Hate Theo. He had given me something miraculous. Only to tear it from my hands and my heart before I could even touch our precious little baby. Was he satisfied now? He'd broken me completely. Me, his enemy's daughter, was now a defenseless whimpering mass of pain and tears.

No doubt he was laughing behind that closed door, delighting in the fact that he didn't have to be stuck with me as his child's mother.

I was so lost in the bitterness and sorrow, crying so hard and loud, I didn't even hear the door opening. I didn't realize I wasn't alone until a soft hand touched my cheek. Gasping in fright, I looked up to find Raven sitting on the edge of my bed, a tissue in her hand as she mopped up my tears.

"I'm not here to hush you or tell you everything is going to be okay," she told me in a quiet voice. "I only came in here to let you know you aren't alone. So, go ahead and cry. Yell and scream. Throw things, if that's what helps. No one is going to judge or condemn you for feeling like the world is against you. It's not, but it probably feels like that right now. You're in my home now, Tavia. You're safe, and I promise you I will protect you until my last breath if that is what it takes."

I frowned up at her through my tears. "Why? You don't know me."

"You remind me of my daughter. That same fire, that same brokenness that lives inside her, I see it in your eyes. And if you believe nothing else, believe that I would give up my life for her. Just as I would for you." She wiped away a few more of my tears. "It's okay to be pissed. It's even okay to hate everyone. To think no one cares... But I do. I'll be right here in your corner, because I can tell that's what you need more than anything else right now. You came here for a reason, but you're mine now."

"But...you just met me," I reminded her, bewildered.

"The first time I met Lexa, my daughter, I took one look at her and knew she was mine. Didn't matter that I didn't give birth to her. Didn't matter that I was hurt and pissed at her dad at the time. She was this tiny little thing who looked up at me like she wanted me to see her, but wasn't sure at the same time. You, I can tell you don't want anyone to see you. That must have worked well for you over the years, kept you under the radar. But I can also tell you need someone to see you, sweetheart. I've accepted you as mine, and you should too." Giving me a smile, she wiped away some more of my tears. "So, welcome to the family. You now have a sister and a brother. I come along with some growly uncles and some pretty amazing aunts, and a shitload of cousins."

Bemusedly, a tiny laugh escaped me. "You're kind of crazy, aren't you?"

"No one has ever called me crazy before. I tend to intimidate people too much for them to say that to my face." She picked up the tray from the side table and placed it back across my lap. "You're all snotty right now, but you still need to eat some of this. Come on, blow your nose, and then take a few bites.

Getting your strength back is priority number one for now."

I surprised myself by doing as she instructed. I blew my nose, grimacing in pain because even that made me hurt. Abdominal pain had to be the worst physical pain imaginable. Simply breathing gave me issues. I didn't know how I was going to handle it when I eventually sneezed or coughed.

Once I was cleaned up, she lifted the bowl and fed me several bites. It looked disgusting, yet even with it having cooled off, it was pretty good. But six spoonsful later and I couldn't handle any more.

A pleased smile teased at her lips as she stood. "Good job. I honestly didn't think you would get that much down. Sit tight. I'll be back in a few to help you to the bathroom."

She was gone for less than five minutes before she was back, but she didn't come alone. A woman with pretty blue eyes and hair just as short as Raven's, only brown, followed her into my room.

"I'm not exactly as strong as I once was," Raven said with a twist of her lips. "So, Flick is going to help me assist you to the bathroom."

Flick looked down at me with so much tenderness in her eyes, I felt the sting of tears in my sinuses return. "Hi, Tavia. You can call me Flick or Felicity. I'm cool with either."

"I... Okay." I felt both shy and defensive, and for some reason, I didn't want to feel either around these two women. They had been kind to me, taking care of me, and Raven had even said I was hers — whatever that meant. I didn't want them to see me as a bitch or as some meek little thing they had to protect from the big bad world.

"How do you want to do this, Rave?" Flick asked the other woman. "I don't want to cause her more pain than we have to."

Raven picked up a pillow and told me to hold it against my stomach. "You hold it there, and we're going to pull you to the edge of the bed. Then you can shift your legs over the side, and we will help you stand. Got it?"

I nodded and clenched the pillow to my stomach, my muscles already tensing to brace for the pain. It was over in a handful of seconds, with minimal discomfort, but if I was relieved that it hadn't been so bad, I had given myself false hope for the rest of the trip to the bathroom.

By the time I got back to the bed, I was exhausted and praying I didn't have to use the toilet again for a good long while. I'd been able to clean up a little, though. Wash and brush my teeth, plus change my clothes. I was in a pair of pajamas that Raven said belonged to her daughter. They fit me pretty well, even if they were a bit long on me, but they were soft and comfortable.

As I shifted back against the pillows of my freshly made bed, there was a knock on the door, quickly followed by the door opening. But the person on the other side only stuck her head in.

Dark hair fell over one side of her face, but I could easily make out her features. I had never seen eyes so clear and blue. When her gaze landed on Raven, something in them softened, just as Raven's green ones did when she looked at the young woman.

"Hey, Mom. You need any help in here? Theo said you were helping the patient freshen up."

"We're almost done in here, sweetheart." Raven tucked the blankets around me before picking up the hairbrush she'd set on the bedside table moments before. "Come in and meet Tavia."

When she walked all the way into the room and approached the bed, I felt the full effect of her. She was tall, practically a giant compared to me, and even Raven. She had to be at least six feet tall, but she was slender and had the body of a supermodel. She was so beautiful that when she tossed her hair back from her face and I saw the scar on her cheek, I didn't even react. Not even that scar could distract from her beauty.

"Hello, Tavia," she greeted, holding out her hand to me. Her left hand, which had a gorgeous engagement ring on it and a matching wedding ring to go with it. "I'm Lexa Davis."

I shook her hand, feeling oddly at ease with her. What was it about these women that I felt like I actually belonged there? It was so natural to relax and accept that they wouldn't hurt, or let anything else hurt, me.

"Is Ben working?" Raven asked as she sat beside me on the bed and started brushing my hair. The first stroke had me briefly closing my eyes in pleasure. No one had ever taken care of me like this before, not even when I was a little girl.

"He actually had an errand to run for Dad," she said. "But he's going to meet me here." Smiling down at me, Lexa shook her head a little exasperatedly. "My husband is the sheriff."

That had me blinking up at her in surprise, making her laugh. "Yeah, that's the look I get every time I tell new people who I'm married to."

"But..." I glanced at the door, wondering if Theo was safe here. After seeing him kill not one but two men, I knew he was into some shady things. And as much as I hated him, I didn't want him to get into trouble.

"Don't worry. Ben is well aware of the darker sides to my friends and family," Lexa assured me. "Theo is perfectly fine. If anything, he should fear Mom more than Ben. Or anyone else, for that matter."

"Lexa," Raven said with a slight warning in her tone. "Don't freak the girl out, honey."

"Right, so is there anything you need? I can run to the store or to the shop if you need me to handle anything for Dad."

"We have everything handled, sweetheart. Thank you, though." Raven finished brushing the tangles out of my hair and stood. "How is your pain level, Tavia?"

"I don't want any narcotics," I told her.

"That wasn't my question," she said with a sternness that had me mumbling that I was hurting pretty badly, especially after all the movement I'd done earlier. "Okay, then. I think you should have a dose of pain medication."

"I don't want it," I told her stubbornly.

"You can't rest properly if you're in this much pain. At least for the next day or so, you should let me give you the medication. Then we can talk to Doc about something lighter."

"I remember you complaining about taking the pain meds after your hysterectomy last year," Lexa commented.

"Hush up, you," Raven muttered. "This is different. She can't even breathe deeply right now because of the pain. Look at how shallowly she's breathing. I'm going to have to talk to Doc about some oxygen until she can breathe a little easier without so much pain."

She wasn't wrong, and I wasn't about to argue with her if it meant getting more oxygen with less effort.

"You're the expert," Lexa told her mom.

"Hang tight, sweetheart. I'll get you taken care of." Promising to return shortly, Raven left, and then it was just Lexa and me since Flick had gone out after she and Raven had helped me to bed.

"You're in great hands," Lexa told me. "And I'm not saying that just because she's my mom. She's already got Theo pouting in a corner because he's been forbidden to come in here until you give the okay. I've known Theo a long time, and only a few people on the planet can actually make him do what they tell him to."

My heart contracted painfully, thinking of Theo. Twisting my fingers in the blankets to give myself something to do besides sitting there looking helpless, I pretended like she hadn't brought him up. "It's pretty quiet around here, huh?"

Lexa laughed. "Considering my brother, Garret, and Nova are at school, of course it is. This evening, when they've finished their homework and Garret is getting into trouble, you'll rethink that. Then there is always the chance that one of the cousins will come over. If Aunt Willa stops by, then at least one of the triplets will tag along." Her lips twisted with amusement and affection. "We have a big family. Something you will see firsthand all too soon, I'm sure."

I nodded like I understood, when the truth was, I had no clue what any of that really meant. A big family wasn't something I understood. A family, period, was only a fantasy to me.

"Theo has told me all about you, actually," Lexa informed me, but if she expected a reaction from me, she was disappointed because I glanced at the window, pretending the sky outside was all the entertainment I needed. "Not just when he called last night to let me know he was coming for an indefinite visit. I mean over the years. He's probably my best friend, so we confide in each other as often as we can. And you have been a topic we've texted about many, many times over the years."

I kept the surprise off my face, but just barely. Why would Theo tell this woman about me? I wasn't anything more than one of the easiest lays he'd ever had. I was nothing to him.

Less than nothing.

NINE

THEO

Creswell Springs was a small town in Northern California. There wasn't a lot of traffic, especially in the part of town where Raven lived. It made it eerily quiet, which was like night and day compared to New York.

The quietness could be either peaceful or too loud, just depended on the person and the situation.

A beer in my hand, standing on the front porch overlooking the neighborhood, I decided that quiet was deafening, making me edgy and restless. Tilting the bottle back, I took a swallow even as my eyes took in everything around me, making sure nothing was coming from any direction that could put Tavia in danger.

Hearing a motorcycle in the distance, I lowered my beer, watching and waiting. A minute later, Spider Masterson, the MC's enforcer, rode by. As I stood there in the fading light of the day, he gave me a chin nod in greeting, letting me know he'd seen me but continued on his way home.

From next door, I heard a feminine giggle. "Matt, stop it!" Rory Reid squealed, and I looked up to find two shadows in one of the upstairs bedrooms. "You know I can't stand it when you tickle me."

"Girl, I told you to stop cracking this window," her husband growled.

"I'm the mother of a teenage boy. Stop calling me 'girl,'" she told him with sass. "And it was too hot in here earlier, but I didn't want to turn on the AC." Her voice faded as Matt lowered and no doubt locked the window.

Silence descended on me again, but it was like there was white noise in my head, too much static. Draining my beer, I leaned my head back against the side of the house and watched the sun fade completely. One by one, the streetlights flickered on.

Inside the house, it was surprisingly quiet, but it wasn't eerie like it was outside. Raven had told the three kids that if they got out of hand and made too much noise, she was going to break every electronic in the house. Soon after, her son, Max, had left to go to his cousin Reid's house—where he tended to stay more often than not, from what Lexa had told me over the years.

As for Garret and Nova, Felicity's children, I had no idea what either of them was doing. But when it came to the boy, I preferred him making noise to let me know where the hell he was. Because when he was quiet, he was getting into trouble, and that could mean just about anything.

My phone going off had me straightening. Pulling it out of my pocket, I glanced down at my screen and bit back a curse when I saw it was my sister. Blowing out a long sigh, I hit connect.

"Hey, Sof."

"Don't you hey me, Theo Volkov!" she raged. "What the hell did you get Tavia into?"

"I can't talk about it right now, Sofia," I bit out, already tired of her bitching at me, and it hadn't even been thirty seconds yet. "We can speak about this when I get back to New York."

"And just when will that be?" she demanded. "Daddy said—"

"I know Pops didn't tell you shit, so stop fishing for information," I cut her off. "You know the rules."

"Fuck the rules," she cried. "Tavia is my friend. You never should have pulled her into your bullshit, Theo. Whatever is going on, no doubt it's dangerous. And you can be a selfish bastard when you set your mind on some stupid task you think is more important than other people's feelings or safety."

"Good talk, Sofia. We'll have to do it again sometime."

"Theo!" Her screaming my name had me pausing from hanging up on her. Lifting the phone back to my ear, I waited. "Stay safe," she said softly, a small quiver in her voice. "I love you. Please be careful."

"I love you too, Sof," I told her. "I'll see you soon, okay?"

"Yeah," she muttered, and then the line went silent.

Releasing the breath I'd been holding, I dropped my hand to my side, clenching my fingers around the phone. I loved my sister, but she was more than a handful at times. She was full of fire and reckless when she got upset. Pops tried to rein her in, but not even he was entirely successful.

Grabbing the empty beer bottle, I walked into the house. The television was on in the living room, but no one was in there watching it. The kitchen was empty too. Tossing the bottle into the recycling, I headed upstairs, but I stopped outside Tavia's door.

It was quiet in the hall, and I strained to hear anything from the other rooms. I could hear a tapping noise from Garret's room. It was rhythmic and annoying, but not so loud that it was easily noticed unless someone was listening for it. From Nova's room, I heard her talking softly, but I didn't hear another voice and figured she was on the phone.

I heard random movement from two other rooms, but Tavia's was completely silent.

She was alone in there and most likely asleep.

Knowing this was the only chance I would get to see her, I quietly opened the door and stepped in. The bedroom was in darkness, but the bathroom door was cracked open with the light on, giving the room just enough illumination to let me see Tavia lying on her back, her eyes closed as she slept.

There were oxygen tubes in her nose, helping her breathe. Raven told me earlier that she needed to speak to the doctor who made house calls for the MC and get the order placed for it since Tavia's pain was making breathing hard for her. The doctor had come, checked her over, and left after setting up the new machine that sat quietly beside her bed.

On the way out, he spoke to me, reassuring me Tavia was doing well, and with Raven looking after her, she would be in the best of hands.

I stepped closer to the bed, my eyes eating up the sight of her. Even pale and fragile-looking, she was the most beautiful woman I'd ever set eyes on. That long dark hair that was so thick it curtained her when it fell into her face. The doe eyes that were so dark when I looked into them while I was deep inside her, I felt like I was falling into an abyss I couldn't climb out of until she whispered my name. Full, kissable lips, straight, cute nose, and the slightest dimple in her chin that combined made up a face I would never get tired of staring at for hours.

Balling my hands into fists to keep from reaching for her, I turned to go, not wanting to disturb her sleep.

Before I could take a step, I heard her shifting, and then a tiny moan escaped her. "No," she breathed, and I turned back to her. "No. Don't touch me. No. No. No!"

Dropping down onto the edge of her bed, I cupped her jaw in my hand. "Tavia," I murmured softly, and her eyes snapped open, her breathing labored despite the oxygen tubes in her nose. Fear marred her beautiful face as her gaze darted around, frantically trying to figure out where she was. "It's okay, krasotka. You're safe, baby."

"Y-Yerik," she panted. "He... I couldn't...get away. He tried..." Tears spilled over her lashes. "And I couldn't..."

The memory of her shirt torn, exposing her bra, Yerik touching her, and then me putting a bullet in his head flashed before my eyes. Renewed rage filled me, and I ached to kill him again. In that moment, I knew how easy it was to hate someone so much that you would want their entire line annihilated. I wanted to wipe out every member of Yerik's family for what he'd done to Tavia.

I rubbed my thumb over her bottom lip, still slightly swollen, the cut having already scabbed over. The bruise along her jaw had changed colors, but it would be a while before it completely faded.

"It's okay," I told her again, but I knew they were empty words to her when she started to tremble so hard, she whimpered in pain. Taking her hands in both of mine, I lifted them to my lips, kissing each hand. "Yerik is dead. He can never touch you again."

"Y-you killed him," she whispered, her brow pinching with confusion. "Y-you saved me. Why?"

"Because I fucking love you more than life itself. Seeing Yerik's hands on you drove me crazy with rage and possessiveness." I wiped away her tears with the pad of my thumb. "You belong to me and only me. You are mine to love and protect."

And I was doing a shit job of both. The woman I cared about the most in the world was lying there, scared and in pain, not believing that I loved her, and it was all my fault.

"Theo." She swallowed with difficulty, but the fear was no longer on her face, and the trembling was slowly starting to fade. "Will you...hold me?"

She didn't have to ask me twice. That she wanted me to hold her, touch her at all, was more than I could have asked for. Standing, I kicked off my shoes and slid into the bed beside her.

Tavia hesitantly pillowed her head on my chest, and I carefully wrapped my arms around her, afraid

I would hurt her. Almost shyly, she placed her hand across my stomach as she tried to get comfortable. I just lay there, letting her shift until she found the right spot. A soft sigh left her, and a few minutes later, her breathing evened out and I knew she was asleep once again.

Pressing my lips to her brow, I closed my eyes. But as soon as I did, I knew it was the wrong thing to do. I hadn't slept in more than forty-eight hours, and the feel of her in my arms felt so damn good that my muscles started to relax one by one and the exhaustion caught up with me.

TEN

The next thing I knew, Raven was touching my shoulder. "Theo," she murmured.

My eyes snapped open, and I quickly looked at Tavia, making sure she was okay. She was sound asleep beside me, her face relaxed as she cuddled into my side, her hand still lying across my lower stomach.

"She's fine," Raven assured me. "I gave her another dose of pain medication about an hour ago, and she fell right back to sleep."

"What time is it?" I glanced at the window, but it was still dark out, so that didn't tell me anything about the time.

"Just after five. I didn't want to wake you, but Bash is going to work and wants to talk to you before he leaves." She walked to the end of the bed. "Go ahead. I've got Tavia covered."

Nodding, I carefully untangled myself from around Tavia. But before I stood, I kissed her brow. She sighed softly and turned her head away, her lashes not even flickering as she continued to sleep peacefully.

"The more sleep she gets at this point, the better. Her body needs time to recover, and as long as she's awake and constantly shifting around, the harder it is for that to happen." Raven patted me on the arm as I walked past her. "You look like shit, by the way. I made coffee, and Flick is making breakfast."

Downstairs, the smell of coffee was too much to resist, and I grabbed a mug. When I turned around, Bash and Jet were both sitting at the kitchen table. Felicity stood at the stove, platters of bacon and pancakes already loaded up.

"How do you like your eggs, Theo?" she asked as she placed another pancake on a plate.

"Whatever is easiest for you, Mrs. Hannigan," I told her.

"Sit," Bash instructed, lifting his own mug of coffee to his mouth. "Talked to your dad just now."

"And?" I asked, taking a seat across from the two men.

"Someone broke in to the girl's dorm room last night. Tore the place up, but there was nothing there to tell them where she might be." He leaned back in his chair, his long dark hair falling over his shoulders. "He also said he would be talking to you later about his security. Apparently he has discovered two other moles who work for Petrov."

"Not surprised," I said with a shrug.

"You were right to bring the girl here," Jet commented, sipping his coffee. "Especially if your father is having difficulties with his men. Your mother and sister should come out here too."

"Mom isn't one to hide," I told him, feeling the hint of a grin teasing at my lips. "Besides, Anya won't let anything happen to her or Sofia."

Three plates of food were placed on the table, all of them full of bacon, pancakes, and scrambled eggs. Jet kissed his wife when she started to move away, thanking her for breakfast. She winked at him and walked back to the stove, humming softly to herself.

I picked up my fork and began eating, my stomach growling angrily with hunger. Before I was finished with my meal, Bash left, and Jet went to wake up his kids. Minutes later, Nova walked into the kitchen, her long blond hair braided down her back.

She looked almost nothing like her mom. Instead, she was the spitting image of her aunt Raven. "Mom, I kept hearing a weird tapping noise coming from Garret's room all night," she complained as she took a seat at the table.

"I'm sure it was nothing," Felicity murmured, not really paying attention to her daughter as she plated pancakes and bacon. Placing the dish in front of Nova, she walked back to the stove.

"But Mom, it was really annoying." From the time she was three, Nova and her brother had spent every summer in New York. I'd gotten to know her more than Garret because she was always following my cousin Ryan around, so I knew that she wasn't much of a complainer—except when it came to her brother.

"He's always doing something to annoy us all, sweetheart. Haven't you learned by now your brother thrives on irritating you?"

Nova muttered something under her breath that made me have to fight a grin. Finishing off my coffee, I stood and carried my dirty dishes to the sink.

"You don't have to do that, Theo," Felicity said. "I've got this. You go check on Tavia. If she's hungry, I can make her another tray with broth and maybe some Jell-O today."

Upstairs, I passed Garret's room and heard Jet in there with his son. "You cannot keep that thing in the house, boy. What the hell? If your mom saw this, she would skin us both alive."

"Ah, come on, Dad. It's not that bad. And look, I built a cage for it."

"Is that the tapping noise your sister was complaining about?" Jet demanded, sounding exasperated. "Damn it, Garret, you cannot have a fucking raccoon in the house. It's a wild animal."

"It's only a baby. I'll take care of it. Mom won't freak as much as you think. She'll think it's cute."

Shaking my head as father and son continued to argue, I opened Tavia's door. She was still in bed, sound asleep. Raven was checking on her oxygen machine and then the IV site that was still in the back of her hand but wasn't connected, although there was a pole with fluids hanging from it in case she did need it.

As I entered the room, Raven glanced my way. "She's been sleeping, but the rest hasn't been nearly as peaceful as when you were in bed with her."

"She had a nightmare yesterday evening. That was why I was in bed with her. She wanted me to hold her." I crossed to the bed and bent to brush my lips over her brow. As my lips touched her forehead, she sighed softly and buried her head deeper into the pillow.

"About the shooting?" Raven asked, her eyes narrowed.

"No," I muttered as I straightened. "It was about what happened before she was shot. Yerik was a member of my father's security. He was actually one of my Mom's personal guards. She had him drive Tavia sometimes." I gritted my teeth, remembering the bastard's hands on her. "He tried to rape her."

"Fuck." Seething now, Raven walked to the end of the bed, her hands clenched at her sides. "I need to teach her some self-defense. Once she's healed, Lexa and I will take care of that."

"I'll teach her." I should have already done that. Anya had taught Sofia and my two female cousins how to protect themselves, so I'd never really had to worry about them knowing what to do if some guy got out of hand—not that they were around guys who weren't family often. But I should have been teaching Tavia self-defense from the first day we'd met.

"You should have already been teaching her," Raven snapped, voicing my same thoughts. "You had your chance. Now I'll do what you haven't. As soon as she's cleared for physical activity, Lexa and I will teach her everything she needs to know about protecting herself."

Before I could argue, my phone went off. The sound made Tavia shift restlessly, and I quickly silenced it before checking to see who it was. Seeing Pops's name on my screen, I walked out of the room so I wouldn't disturb her before answering.

"Hey, Pops," I greeted as I walked downstairs.

"Reid tell you about Tavia's dorm room?" he asked before I'd even reached the front door.

"Yeah. Did they take anything?"

He grunted. "Her laptop is missing, and it looked like a few pictures had been taken from her desk. The one of her and Sofia wasn't in her room, and I know for a fact that she had that picture because I saw it when I took Sofia to visit her there once."

I clenched my fingers around the phone. "They could target Sof next to try to find out where Tavia is."

"I know, son. For now, she is still at Anya's. She's not going anywhere but school and back there, and even when she is at school, Ciro has two men watching over her since they are already there for Zariah."

Relieved that my sister was covered, I leaned one of my forearms on the porch banister and glared off into the distance. "Do you think Tavia is safe here? Is this too close?"

I hated how unsure I sounded, but I needed to know if I was doing the right thing. Tavia was my top priority. Her safety was all that mattered to me. And even though we were on the other side of the country now, I felt like she was still too close to danger.

"Honestly? I don't think there is any place truly safe for Tavia right now. They want her, Theo. And they want her badly. She's the last of the Bykov bloodline. Adas will do anything to take her out. He wants her more than he wants you, and you killed his brother. It won't matter to him that he will be starting a war with me and Anya over this. His hatred for the Bykov family is too strong for him to give a fuck about anything else." He blew out a long breath, sounding just as tired as I felt. "But as things stand, you have her in the safest place I can imagine at the moment. Just keep your eyes open, trust your gut, and know that I have your back no matter what."

ELEVEN

Frustrated, I jerked the oxygen out of my nose and scooted to the edge of the bed.

I was tired of sleeping all day, tired of feeling helpless and reliant on everyone, tired of my nose being dry and irritated due to the flow of air from the oxygen tubes. I hadn't had to have the hard pain medication in more than twenty-four hours, and my stomach muscles didn't hurt nearly as badly as they once had.

But the women were still telling me to rest, only letting me up when I needed to use the bathroom. Considering all they were feeding me was freaking broth, Jell-O, and protein shakes, my stomach was fucking empty, and all I wanted was a big juicy burger. Yet when I told them I was hungry, the only thing I got was that stupid bone broth shit that might taste good but did nothing to fill the gnawing hunger in my gut.

When I got cranky or downright bitchy with any of them, they grinned like they were happy I'd complained and snapped at them. As if they thought I was fragile when I wasn't yelling in their direction. And no matter how loud I screamed or shouted, Theo never reacted.

I didn't get the grins from him that Raven or Flick or Lexa gave me when I was bitching. I didn't get the snarky comebacks or the cajoling when I was being stubborn. He held me when I woke up from a nightmare, he told me he loved me when he kissed my brow and then commanded me to sleep.

But when I woke up, he would be gone.

Every damn time.

Not that I wanted to talk to him. Or see him. I hated him—mostly.

I could feel the tension in him, yet he wouldn't tell me what was wrong. And I refused to beg him to confess. I was done asking for his attention. Done begging for anything where Theo Volkov was concerned. His words of love were empty anyway.

Slowly, I pushed to my feet and waited. For the burn. For the dizziness. For anything that would tell me I was overdoing it and that maybe Raven was right to tell me I needed to stay in bed a little longer. The pain was only a fraction of what it had been, more discomfort than actual pain at this point, and the dizziness was nonexistent.

My muscles were stiff and weak when I walked into the bathroom, making the process a little slower without someone to assist me. Once I was in there, I took care of business and then washed up. But my hair felt limp, and my entire body was sticky, even though I'd had a quick shower with Raven's and Flick's help only the day before.

I turned on the water and stripped while it warmed up. Stepping into the tub, I tipped my head back to the spray and let it flood over me. It felt so good, I couldn't fight the moan that left me.

By the time I was done washing my hair, I was exhausted, but a feeling of accomplishment filled me. I felt the ghost of a smile teasing at my lips when I finally turned off the water.

Pushing back the curtain, I reached for the towel, only to find Theo standing there holding it. His eyes darkened when they skimmed over me, hunger ravaging his face. Gasping in surprise, I stepped back, and I felt my foot slide out from under me. With a whimper, I felt myself start to fall, and my muscles tensed, waiting for the impact of pain when I hit the ground.

Theo's arms going around me and taking all of my weight saved me. I was pulled out of the tub and swung into his arms, still soaking wet but suddenly breathless from his closeness.

"Are you okay, krasotka?" he murmured softly, his lips brushing over my brow before he placed me carefully on my feet and wrapped the towel around my damp body. "Does anything hurt?"

Still stunned, I shook my head, holding the towel to my chest to hide my nakedness from him. Theo was the epitome of male perfection, from his face to those chiseled abs to his muscular thighs. Hell, even his feet were oddly perfect, something I'd only noticed once, when our legs were entangled right after we'd had sex for the first time.

And I was anything but perfect. My breasts were too small, my hips too wide, my stomach too soft in places. And now there were scars everywhere, not only from being shot, but also from the surgery that saved my life. My abdomen looked like someone had tried to play that children's game Operation with it and then sewn me up once they were done.

"You should have waited for me or one of the women to help you shower," he grumbled. "You aren't well enough to handle things like this on your own yet, baby."

Being scolded by him helped shake off the shock, and I glared up at him. "I'm not a child. I have been taking care of myself all my life, Theo. And I'm fine now. I can do things on my own." Tucking the towel into place, I grabbed a second one to wrap around my hair and pushed past him to return to the bedroom.

I'd come to this house with nothing but the clothes Theo's aunt had supplied for me. Since then, Lexa had donated all my other clothing needs, but hers were all considerably longer on me than I was used to. Still, I was thankful for them as I pulled on a pair of fresh panties and then slid on a pair of yoga pants before reaching for a T-shirt.

A bra was one thing Lexa couldn't offer since we weren't exactly the same size in the chest department, so I'd been without one all week. Having been stuck in bed, I hadn't really given it much thought. But now that I planned on doing anything other than lying around being lazy, I probably needed to figure out something to contain my breasts. They might not have been anything to take note of, but without a bra, people would definitely notice.

As I pulled the T-shirt into place, I dropped the towel. I was sore after all the activity of showering and dressing, not to mention nearly falling, so I was moving a little slower as I walked toward the door.

"Where do you think you're going?" Theo demanded from behind me.

I didn't even bother to glance back at him. "To talk to Raven or Flick about getting a bra."

A choking sound coming from him had me pausing with my hand on the doorknob, and I looked at him over my shoulder. "What?"

"You haven't said anything about needing a bra," he half growled, his eyes going straight to my chest and the simple pink T-shirt that was the only thing covering my breasts.

"That's because I was lying in bed for days and didn't consider it. Now that I'm able to move around, I need one." Opening the door, I walked through and hurried to the stairs.

The house was a lot bigger than I'd imagined. I had been asleep when we arrived, so I hadn't seen anything but the room I'd been trapped in for a week. Pictures decorated the wall and were angled along the stairs as I descended them to the first floor.

I heard voices and followed them. The living room was large and homey. A picture of Lexa in her wedding dress standing with her parents was on the mantel. I hadn't met her father yet, but I wasn't surprised to find she looked so much like him.

Pushing open the door to the kitchen, I found Raven standing at the island. A smaller woman with gray eyes stood beside her, both of them chopping vegetables. The new woman's hair was just as short as Raven's and Flick's, making me wonder if the pixie style was something everyone favored in this part of the country.

Both women looked at me as I entered the room.

"I was wondering when you were going to chance getting up," Raven said with a grin as she carried her cutting board to the stove and tossed the peppers she'd just chopped into a pot.

"You told me not to," I reminded her, unable to completely hide the pout in my tone.

"Of course I did. But I've also learned how stubborn you are. I knew once you were actually ready to get up, you would, whether I said you could or not." She returned to the island and started on an onion. "How about some mashed potatoes for dinner?"

My stomach growled hungrily. "With gravy?" I asked hopefully, disliking how young and unsure I sounded.

Raven smiled. "If that's what you want."

I nodded, my gaze going back to the other woman, who was watching me even as she chopped her own pile of peppers.

"Tavia, this is Lexa's aunt, Willa Masterson," Raven introduced.

"It's good to finally meet you, Tavia." Willa wiped her hands on a dish towel and walked over to me, her hand extended. I shook it, noting how strong her grip was. "We've all been worried about you, but Raven refused to let anyone except Flick or Lexa up so you weren't overwhelmed."

"We're making cheesesteak soup," Raven informed me as she sliced the onions. "Unfortunately, you can't have any quite yet, but I'll freeze some for you. So when you finally can eat it, it will be ready."

"You don't have to do that," I murmured, even though my stomach was begging me for a bowl then and there. I'd never had cheesesteak soup, but it sounded amazing. "I don't want to be a bother."

"No bother. Willa and I are making enough to feed everyone. Saving you a little is nothing." Her brows pulled together when she looked behind me, and I didn't have to turn to know Theo had come into the kitchen.

I'd felt him as soon as the door opened. There had always been something about him, some aura or magnetism that alerted me to his nearness.

Fighting not to shiver, I walked to the fridge and extracted a bottle of water, anything to avoid looking at him. "Actually, there was something I needed to ask you," I spoke to Raven. "I seem to be in need of a bra."

"What size are you?" Willa was the one to ask, her eyes on my chest. "You look like a B cup."

"Thirty-eight B," I told her and she nodded.

"Perfect. That's what my girls wear. I'll call over to the house and have one of them bring a few." She picked up her phone that was lying on the island beside her chopping board and dialed. "Monroe, I need you to grab a few of your bras and bring them over to Aunt Raven's. Thanks, sweetheart." With a smile, she went back to chopping. "She just got home from school. She'll be over in a few."

"I will send Lexa to the mall and get you whatever you need," Theo said as he pulled a beer from the fridge. "Clothes, underwear, bras, and anything else you want."

It was that easy. All he had to do was throw money at whatever problem got in his way. That was exactly what I expected him to do, but I didn't want a single cent of his money spent on me.

"No, I don't need, nor do I want, new things." It wasn't like I was used to new things anyway. Growing up, all my clothes had come from boxes of clothing donated to the home I lived in. Then once I was out on my own, I saved all the money I could by getting the items I did happen to need from secondhand stores.

"Tavia—" Theo started to argue, but I didn't want to hear what he was about to say. No doubt it would only piss me off or hurt me. Either way, I wasn't willing to hear what was about to come out of his mouth.

I shook my head at him, disturbing the towel wrapped around my damp hair. Blowing out a heavy sigh, I pulled off the towel and rewrapped it around my thick hair. It would take hours for it to air-dry, but I didn't have the energy to blow-dry the heavy locks.

"Flick went to pick up the kids from school," Raven commented. "But when she gets back, she can help you with your hair if you want."

"Thank you, but it's fine. I'll just let it air-dry." And I wasn't going to care if it got frizzy or turned into a mop. It wasn't like I had anyone I needed to impress with straight hair that didn't look like a pack of rats lived in it. Least of all Theo.

"I'll help you," he offered in his deep voice from right beside me, causing me to jump. I hadn't expected him to be so close, and when I turned my head, it was to find him less than a foot away. He lifted one of his huge hands, touching my towel, and for a moment, my heart skipped a beat. But then I remembered I hated him and jerked my head back. "I know how much you dislike letting your hair go untamed."

"It's fine," I repeated between clenched teeth. It wasn't so much that I didn't want to accept help; I just didn't want to be a bother.

But Theo helping me could not happen, no matter what. I couldn't let him touch me. Every brain cell in my head seemed to go on vacation when he was close enough to touch. If his hands were on me, even innocently helping me dry my hair, I would melt for him like a popsicle dissolving into a sticky mess on the sidewalk in August.

I couldn't let him have that much control over my body when I was still weak from being shot.

TWELVE

The back door that led into the kitchen opened. I turned to find a beautiful girl, no more than fifteen, walking into the house. Her hair was long, a lighter brown color, and her eyes the same shade of gray as Willa's. Dressed in jeans and a pastel pink shirt, she looked sweet and innocent.

In her hand, she was carrying a Victoria's Secret bag, which she placed on the table. "I got a few different styles. You didn't say who it was for or why, so I didn't know which ones would be more comfortable," the girl said in a voice that was musically soft.

"Thanks, honey," Willa said, continuing her chopping. "Tavia, this is my youngest, Monroe. Mon, this is Tavia."

A shy smile lifted at her lips, and she waved. "Hi," she murmured in that voice that made me want to sit down and just listen to her talk for hours.

"Hi," I greeted. "Thank you for the bra selection."

"So, they're for you," she said with a brighter smile. "I thought they were going to be for one of Max's girlfriends or something."

Raven snorted. "Like he would bring one of them home."

"True," Monroe agreed with a laugh. "But you never know around here."

The back door opened again, and I had to blink a few times when another girl walked in. This girl was the same height and build as Monroe, her eyes the same shade of gray, and there was no mistaking that this was Monroe's twin. They looked so alike it was disconcerting. But even though I suspected they were identical, it was very easy to tell who was who.

The new girl's hair was jet-black, no doubt dyed, although it looked good on her. She had a distinctive style, a kind of punk-rocker vibe going on with her shredded shirt and distressed jeans. Where Monroe's face was devoid of makeup, the other girl's eyes were heavily made-up, making the gray stand out more. Her nails were painted black, and several leather and beaded bracelets dangled from her wrists.

"Mom, Maverick said he was going to be late," she said as she walked to the fridge and pulled out a can of Diet Coke. Closing the door with her hip, she popped the top and tipped back the can, drinking it thirstily.

Willa sighed heavily. "Of course he is. That boy is going to make me a grandmother if he's not careful," she grumbled. Shaking her head, she tossed her chopped peppers into the pot on the stove. "Tavia, this is my other daughter, Mila. I would like to introduce you to their brother, but apparently he's somewhere dicking around."

"With River," Mila told her, a wicked gleam in her eyes.

"Ah fuck," Willa groaned, while Raven laughed.

"Told you," was all the blonde said to the other woman before wiping her hands on a clean dish towel. "Girls, take Tavia upstairs and help her dry her hair. She's still sore, so she needs some assistance with the hair dryer."

"Sure thing, Aunt Raven," Monroe readily agreed.

Mila eyed my hair in the towel then shrugged. "Yeah, I don't have anything else going on. Let's go play hair and makeup."

I wanted to protest, but Monroe took my hand and started tugging me toward the door. "Mila, grab the VS bag. Tavia can try on all the bras I brought over for her."

"So, they're for her? That's cool. I thought maybe they were for one of Max's slutty girlfriends or something." She picked up the bag and followed us out of the room. "Mom jokes and says Maverick is going to get River pregnant, but I think Aunt Raven is the one who should be worried about becoming a grandmother before her dumb-ass son finishes high school."

"I don't think Mom is worried as much about Mav and River getting pregnant as she is about Uncle Colt killing Maverick for having sex with his daughter," Monroe told her twin.

"True. But River is only fourteen. She shouldn't be having sex anyway."

"Maverick is only fifteen, and neither should he."

"Wait." I stopped and turned to face them both at the top of the stairs. "Aren't you two fifteen?"

"Yup," Mila confirmed.

"We're triplets," Monroe explained. "Maverick is the oldest."

"By three minutes," Mila muttered. "And he doesn't let us forget it either. I swear, he acts just like Dad, not letting us do anything fun."

"Our definitions of fun are totally different, Mil," Monroe told her.

"Staying locked in the house all the time is not fun, Mon. I don't care what your definition is."

Laughing at the two of them bickering, I led the way into my room. There was a hair dryer in the cabinet under the sink, and Mila pulled it out before grabbing the brush. "Let's see what we have to work with, Tavia," she said as she plugged the dryer into the outlet beside the bed.

I took the towel off my head and shook out my hair, letting it fall down my back.

"Well, hell," Mila said with a shake of her head. "No wonder you need help. My arms would get tired having to dry all of that mess too, and I don't even have a gunshot wound to deal with."

"Mil," Monroe scolded.

"What?" the other girl grumbled. "It's not like she thought we didn't know." Her gray gaze went to me. "Don't worry, though, Tavia. We haven't told anyone about you. We know better than to talk about MC business to outsiders."

I sat up a little straighter, but I gave her a small smile. "I wasn't worried." And for some reason, I wasn't. Oddly enough, I trusted everyone in this house, most of whom I hadn't even really met yet.

It took a while, but the two sisters did a great job on my hair. After they were finished, my hair felt softer and thankfully wasn't a static-filled wreck that resembled an angry cat that had just been struck by lightning.

Monroe stood in front of me, straightening up the mess the two had made while blow-drying my hair. When she bent forward to pick up the towel off the bed, her necklace fell forward, and the charm she'd kept tucked under her shirt came out. It was a silver medallion, but I couldn't make out what it was.

On instinct, I reached out, grasping it so I could take a closer look.

"It's Saint Michael," Monroe told me, pulling the chain from me and tucking the charm back into her shirt.

"It's from her stalker," Mila commented, making me look at her in surprise. "And she never takes it off."

"Mila!" Monroe hissed at her.

"What? Like Mom doesn't know you wear that thing as a talisman."

"But she doesn't know where I got it," Monroe muttered.

"Neither do you. Anyone could have left that thing for you," Mila shook her dark head. "A serial killer could have given it to you, for all you know."

"He's not a serial killer," her sister defended. "Why would a serial killer give me a medallion that is supposed to protect me?"

"I'm not arguing with you over this. I've told you over and over again you're insane for not telling Mom and Dad you have a stalker, but you never listen." Muttering to herself, Mila left the room.

Bemused, I watched the door close behind her.

"Tavia…" Monroe's hesitant voice pulled my gaze back to her. "Please don't tell anyone what Mila just said. He's not really a stalker."

I didn't know if I should be amused, concerned, or frightened for her. But there was a real plea in her voice, and I didn't want to let her down. "He?"

"I don't know his name, but he left me this necklace about a year ago. I came home, and it was just lying on my bed. There was a note that told me to always wear it and I'll always be protected." Her lips pressed into a hard line. "Something had happened not long before that, and we lost some people. My dad was freaking out and wouldn't let Mila or me even leave the house without him or one of my uncles with us. So, I started wearing the necklace. It sounds weird, but it's actually saved me a few times already... Well, not so much the necklace as...him."

"Who is he?" I asked, lowering my voice because hers was so quiet.

Her mouth snapped shut, and she shook her head. "I've already told you too much. Please...just don't say anything to my parents or Aunt Raven. None of them would understand. They wouldn't even try."

"Are you sure you're safe, though?" She looked so upset that I didn't want to push her, but I liked her and I didn't want anything to happen to her.

Something changed in her. I wasn't sure what it was, but something in her eyes was different, her smile softer. It was almost as if she was suddenly glowing. "He would never let anything harm me. If nothing else, I know that."

"But your sister—"

"Is just as bad as my dad and brother. Just because I'm the baby—and only by two minutes—they all act like I can't do anything without someone holding my hand." Frustrated, she blew out a heavy sigh and sat on the edge of the bed beside me. "I'm not helpless."

"They just love you," I tried to soothe, and I surprised myself when I put my arm around her. "They love you and can't stand the thought of something happening to you. You're very lucky, Monroe."

"You're lucky, too. Theo obviously cares about you a lot. I overheard him talking to Lexa on the porch the other night. He said he didn't know what he would have done if you'd died. He wouldn't have wanted to live if you had." Her hand went to her medallion, holding it through her shirt. "I hope a guy loves me that much one day."

THIRTEEN

"Ivan stopped two of Petrov's men from taking Sofia this evening." Pops's voice was low, menacing. Deadly. Considering what he was telling me, I wasn't surprised.

Rage was twisting my gut, making my blood boil. I wanted to wrap my hands around Adas's throat and squeeze until I saw the life fade from his eyes.

The bastard couldn't find Tavia or me, so he was targeting the only other person who might possibly know where his prey was hiding. My baby sister.

"She snuck out to go to a party, and luckily, Ivan followed her. Petrov's men were watching the compound, waiting for their chance, and they nearly fucking had it." The last words ended on a roar, but I just sat there, unflinching and waiting.

"Ivan took a bullet to the shoulder," he continued after a few deep, calming breaths. "He will be fine. Sofia is unharmed, but shaken. Both she and your mom are now very much aware of how dangerous the situation currently is."

"No chatter on if Petrov suspects where Tavia is?" I asked.

"Nothing," he confirmed. "How is she?"

I glanced at the ceiling, picturing Tavia asleep in her bed. She'd had a lot of physical activity earlier in the day compared to the previous week. But by nine o'clock, she'd been exhausted and had crashed while watching television with Raven, Felicity, and Nova on the couch in the living room. I'd carried her up to bed and tucked her in, but after getting the cold shoulder from her almost all day, I left so as not to upset her more if she awoke and found me staring.

"She's feeling better," I assured Pops.

"Good to hear. And how are you doing, son?" he asked after a pause.

I scrubbed a hand over my face, fighting my own exhaustion mixed with frustration and lingering rage after hearing about Sofia's near miss.

How was I?

I didn't fucking know the answer to that question.

Blowing out a frustrated exhale, I told him what was eating at me the most. "I feel like I'm a pussy hiding from the enemy, Pops."

"That's bullshit. A man has to know his priorities, Theo. Loving his woman, protecting her, that has to be his number one. Fuck everything else."

"Eliminating Petrov is the only way to really protect her. Staying here is not solving anything. The longer he's breathing, the longer she's in danger." I stood and paced the living room. Everyone else was in bed, but I couldn't sleep. Most nights, I walked around the first floor of the house, making sure it was secure. I rarely slept, catching an hour here and there whenever Tavia had a nightmare and wanted me to hold her.

"What do you want to do then, son?" he asked.

"I'm coming back," I told him, having already made up my mind. "Tavia will stay here, where it's safer. But I have to take care of Adas myself."

"You're right," Pops admitted. "I'll arrange for you to get back."

We talked for a little longer and then said goodbye. Ten minutes later, I got a text telling me the jet would arrive first thing the next morning. Dropping down onto the couch, I leaned my head back and closed my eyes.

I had to return to New York. Taking care of Adas, making sure Tavia was safe, was the only option. Letting others do what was my job and mine alone, even if it was Pops handling it, wasn't acceptable. But leaving her here, being away from her, was going to tear me apart.

Scrubbing my hands over my face, I stood and climbed the stairs. The lamp on the nightstand was on, casting a soft glow over her and the bed. She was sleeping on her side, one hand tucked under her cheek, making her look young and innocent.

The oxygen was turned off and the machine pushed to a corner of the room, along with the IV pole she hadn't needed. Raven had taken the IV out of Tavia's hand the day before since she was doing so well and didn't need the extra fluids the doctor had provided for her.

Kicking off my shoes, I climbed in behind Tavia and carefully wrapped my arms around her, not wanting to disturb her sleep. She sighed peacefully, then turned over, her face burrowing against my chest.

"Theo," she murmured softly without opening her eyes.

Touching my lips to the top of her head, I closed my eyes, savoring the feel of her in my arms and storing the memory for while I was away from her. I didn't know how long it was going to take to deal with Adas, but I couldn't return for her until he was taken care of. Only when I knew it was safe for her to return to New York would I see her again.

"I have to go, krasotka," I murmured into her hair, knowing she wouldn't hear me but needing to speak the words aloud. "I have to ensure your safety."

She sighed again, snuggling deeper into my warmth.

"When I return for you, we will finally be able to begin our future together. Until then, always remember that I love you."

"Theo?" she whispered, her lashes fluttering upward to show me those darker-than-espresso eyes. "What did you say?"

"Nothing, krasotka," I told her, kissing her brow. "Sleep, baby."

"Okay," she yawned delicately. "Goodnight, Theo."

I held her for hours, refusing to close my eyes even for a second, wanting to soak up every moment of this for later. But when I heard people moving around in the house, getting ready for work, I knew it was time to let her go.

For now, I reminded myself as I carefully untangled myself from her and stood. But I will return for her. Soon.

Letting myself have one more moment to gaze down at her, memorizing her features all over again, I forced myself to turn and walk away.

FOURTEEN

Yawning, I turned over in bed, stretching carefully. When I came into contact with nothing but the chilled other half of the bed, I opened my eyes.

A feeling of déjà vu hit me, and my heart contracted painfully as sadness began to press down on me. I didn't know why, because it wasn't like it was the first time I'd woken up alone after Theo had held me during the night. But I couldn't remember having a nightmare, so I didn't know why he'd been in bed with me this time.

The morning I woke up after Theo and I made love all night in my dorm room, I'd felt a sense of loss as soon as I opened my eyes. I hadn't known right away that it was the last time I would see him for weeks. I'd just thought maybe he hadn't wanted to wake me up before leaving for work.

I'd told myself it was sweet, but in my heart, I knew better. Waking up alone in bed the morning after giving yourself to a guy was not a good thing. Later, when I'd tried to call him and he'd sent me to voice mail, I'd told myself it was okay. He was just busy and would call me back when he got the chance. No way he could make love to me so passionately, as if he couldn't get enough of me, as if it were killing him because he couldn't get close enough, and not feel as strongly as I did.

I told myself that for weeks, my heart breaking a little more with each passing day that he didn't do as I wanted—needed—him to do and call or text. Anything to let me know I meant more to him than a one-night stand. Another notch on his belt. Another conquest that was quickly forgotten as he moved on to the next easy lay.

Upset with myself for letting it get to me again, I got out of bed and dressed. Downstairs, the house felt oddly empty as I walked through the living room and into the kitchen. Flick stood at the sink, doing dishes and humming to herself. When I entered the room, she turned, a smile on her face for me in greeting.

"Good morning. Sleep well?" Picking up a dish towel, she dried her hands. "How about some scrambled eggs for breakfast? Raven said you did so well with the mashed potatoes last night that eggs would be fine today."

"She's not here?" I asked hesitantly, when what I really wanted to ask was where Theo was.

"No, it's just me and you until I have to pick up the kids. Raven has a few things to do today." Pulling out a carton of eggs, she walked to the stove. "So, scrambled?"

"Y-yes please." My voice cracked as I sat at the table.

I didn't need Flick to tell me Theo was gone; I could feel his absence in my soul. The sudden, overwhelming loss, the feeling like he'd abandoned me, made a joke of every time I'd told myself I hated him. Swallowing around the knot in my throat, I forced a smile for Flick as she placed the plate of eggs in front of me.

But I wasn't hungry, so I only picked at my food, pushing it around the plate with my fork and pretending like I was just taking my time eating.

Flick snuck glances at me over her shoulder from the sink, but she didn't comment on it, nor did she offer an explanation of where Theo was.

Maybe she didn't know, and that was why she didn't talk about him. I wanted that to be the case, but instinct told me it wasn't. Most likely, everyone who lived there knew where he was, but apparently I wasn't special enough to be in the loop.

Eventually, I gave up pretending to eat and tossed the food in the trash before taking my empty dish to the sink. Flick's blue eyes were full of understanding and sympathy as she took the plate from me. "It's nice out today. Why don't you sit on the porch and get some sun? It will be good for you."

Nodding dejectedly, I walked through the house and out onto the front porch. There were no chairs, so I sat on the top step, letting the sun beat down on me as I glanced around at the other houses in the neighborhood without really seeing them.

Why did Theo leave? Had something happened, or was he just bored? Maybe now that I was feeling better and able to move around, do things on my own, he figured he didn't have to bother with me anymore.

Maybe the only reason he'd come with me in the first place was because he felt guilty over the baby…

Pain so intense it made me gasp hit me dead center, and I pressed one hand to my heart and the other to my lower abdomen. I hadn't thought about the miscarriage since Theo told me—hadn't allowed myself to think about the baby. Every time I did dwell on what happened, and the precious gift that had been snatched from me before I even had a chance to love my child, I pushed the thoughts back in self-defense against the pain and grief.

But now, with Theo gone, I couldn't hide from it any longer.

Life had grown inside me. A baby that was equal parts Theo and me. I bet it would have been perfect, just like him. I would have loved our precious little baby, would have given it a life so much better than the one I had growing up. A life full of being showered with love and affection. My child never would have known loneliness or felt like they didn't belong in the world. Never would they have felt as if they weren't good enough to be loved.

But I wasn't ever going to get to do any of that. I would never hold my baby, never tell him or her how much I loved them, never shower them with all the love I was aching to give.

Tears spilled from my eyes, and a sob that felt as if it were ripped from my very soul released into the quiet morning. How was it possible to survive this kind of agony? It was worse than anything I'd ever experienced. It was worse than the physical pain of being shot.

All I wanted was to curl up in a ball and die. Maybe then the pain would stop. Maybe then I could be with the baby I'd lost.

What was there for me here in this world anyway?

Nothing and no one.

Theo had left me—again. I had no family, no one who cared if I was alive or dead. Fuck, my own biological father hadn't even wanted me, had given me away and left me to fend for myself. And now what blood I did have wanted me dead.

There was no one who wanted me. No one who needed me.

Maybe...

Maybe it would be better for everyone if I was just...gone.

There had to be a reason my own uncle wanted to wipe out my maternal bloodline. Perhaps we just weren't worth living. Wouldn't it be doing him a favor if I ended this madness already?

The sound of a vehicle approaching pulled me from the torture of my dark inner thoughts. I watched as a Trinity County Sheriff's sport utility vehicle pulled into the driveway. The SUV was turned off, and moments later, a man with short, dark hair and dressed in a police uniform stepped out.

With shoulders practically as wide as the vehicle he'd just climbed out of and eyes a unique reddish golden-brown that took in everything as soon as he was outside, the man was both scary and intriguingly handsome. His stride was easy, like he was used to making the walk up the sidewalk to the front porch, and even though I had yet to meet him, I instantly knew this was Lexa's husband, Ben.

"Morning," he greeted as he walked toward me. "You wouldn't happen to have seen my wife by any chance, would you?"

I shook my head. "I haven't seen anyone but Flick today," I told him in a voice still choked with the tears that had yet to dry on my face. Embarrassed, I scrubbed my hands across the dampness.

"So Raven isn't here either?" I shook my head, and he blew out a resigned sigh. "Figures. I never know what kind of trouble those two are going to get into. Hopefully I won't have to hide a dead body this time, though."

He said it with a grin, but there was something in his eyes that made me wonder if he was actually joking.

"I'm Ben, by the way. No doubt you already knew that, though." His eyes filled with empathy as another tear spilled down my cheek. "And you're Tavia."

"Th-that's me," I told him with a grimace.

He dropped down onto the top step beside me, and he turned so his back was leaning against the banister. "I get why Volkov went back to New York. Whatever is going on, he wants to take care of it personally, make sure you're safe. If it were Lexa, I'd do the same thing. Although leaving her here with her mom while I was across the country without her would be its own kind of hell."

My brows pinched together. It didn't surprise me in the least that a man I'd just met knew where Theo was, and yet I hadn't. It only pushed home all over again that I meant nothing to him. "Whatever reason Theo went back to New York, I didn't even factor into it."

The sheriff's eyes narrowed on me. "You still on those pain killers Lexa was telling me Doc prescribed for you?"

"What?" I stared at him in bewilderment. "No, of course not. I haven't had any pain medication in a few days now."

"Huh. Then you must be high on something else."

"I'm not high," I snapped at him, confused as to why he thought I wasn't lucid. "Why would you think that?"

"Because I might not know Theo as well as Lexa does, but I do know that he's been twisted in knots over you and what's been going on back east." He stood, dusting off his work pants as he descended the steps. "Give him a few days. He'll return for you." On the sidewalk, he paused and glanced back at me. "I need to get to work. Have to make these people think they did the right thing by voting for me. See you around, Tavia. And if you happen to come across my wife, tell her to get her sweet ass home."

FIFTEEN

After the sheriff left, I couldn't stand to be outside. The sun felt too bright, the air too thin, the sounds of the outside world echoing in my head. Going back inside, I asked Flick if there was a computer or tablet I could borrow so I could contact my professors.

School had only been a fleeting thought since being shot, but I couldn't afford to lose my scholarship for nonattendance. I needed to let them know why I wasn't showing up for my classes.

"I think I can find you something," she told me with that warm, maternal, and understanding smile of hers. "Make yourself comfortable, and I'll bring it to you."

I went back to my room and sat on the end of the bed, staring out the window at the sun as it slowly moved across the cloudless sky. A tap on the door was my only warning before the door opened and Flick walked in, carrying an older style iPad in her hand.

"This is Nova's old iPad. She has a phone now and never plays with this thing, so you can use it all you want." Handing it over, she stepped back. "Let me know when you get hungry. We can have lunch together."

"Thanks, Flick," I mumbled, and she gave me a wink before turning and leaving me alone.

Once the door was closed behind her, I turned on the iPad and opened a browser window to check my email. I had to work through the list of things already waiting on me, mostly emails from my other clients asking if I was okay and why I hadn't contacted them or shown up for our usual appointments.

I figured it would be bad for business if I told them I'd been shot and there was a Russian mobster trying to kill me, so I went with a simpler excuse. I was attacked on my way to a client's house and badly hurt. That I was only just now out of bed and able to move around. All of it was true, just not the full story, which I didn't plan on sharing. But I apologized for not contacting them all sooner and promised I would be back on my feet soon before pleading with them not to find a new tutor to take my place.

I would help them via email all I could, so that was a plus, and if push came to shove, I could do video conferences if needed. I couldn't afford to lose even one client, any more than I could the loss of my full-ride scholarship.

Once I had everyone filled in—with the exception of Sofia since I was fairly sure she already knew what was going on—I emailed my professors and gave them the same excuse, hoping they took pity on me and excused my absences without it affecting my grades or the attendance policy that would hinder my funding for the upcoming term.

By the time I was done, I could barely keep my eyes open, and it wasn't even noon yet. I hated being so weak, but apparently I was still recovering. All I wanted to do was sleep. Tossing the iPad aside, I crawled up the bed and slid under the covers, not even bothering to turn off the lights before letting sleep take me.

A firm tap on my bedroom door roused me sometime later. Blinking my eyes open, I saw the sun was starting to go down, and I sat up in bed just as the door opened.

Lexa walked in carrying four large shopping bags, one of which was from Best Buy. Grinning, she walked over to the bed and placed all the bags around me. "Sorry it took so long. The mall is about an hour away, and I had to do a little searching for all the things on Theo's list."

I frowned down at the bags, then up at her. "What's this?"

"Presents from Theo. A new laptop for you to do all your schoolwork on, a new phone, and a few other little things." When I just glared down at the bags, she lost her grin. "What's wrong? You don't like them?"

"I don't want any of this," I told her, and I pushed the bags to the end of the bed without even looking at the contents. "Take them back. Keep them for yourself. Do whatever you want, but I don't want anything from Theo."

"Ah, come on. Don't be like that." She picked up the Best Buy bag and tried to offer it to me. "It's got everything you need. Trust me, because I had them set it up before we left the store. Theo was insistent on every last detail."

"Fuck Theo," I muttered under my breath. "Look, Lexa. I don't want to be a bitch to you, but I don't want anything from Theo. Not his money, not his time, or anything else. Apparently I don't even warrant a goodbye from him, so it's obvious I don't matter to him. And I'm not going to take things he's only offering because he feels guilty."

Tossing back the covers, I got out of bed and walked toward the bathroom. "Please, just take this stuff back or keep it. Honestly, I don't even care what you do with it. Just keep it away from me."

I stayed in the bathroom long after I heard Lexa leave, the rustling of the bags telling me she'd taken them with her. I didn't know what all was in those bags other than the electronics, and I didn't want to know.

If Theo's goal was to soften me up with gifts, he was miles away from hitting the mark. I didn't want his blood money or his gifts to repent for all the sins he'd committed against me. His words of love were nothing, not that I'd believed them to begin with. But if he'd really cared about me—if he'd known me at all—he would have realized that throwing money at me was not how to show me he cared.

Taking a deep breath, I tried to swallow down the lump that was choking me, and I walked back into the bedroom. As I did, there was a sudden noise so loud, it sounded like an explosion, and the house literally shook.

Frightened, I ran to the window to see what had caused it.

Looking down, I saw the back end of what looked like a late model van sticking out of the front of the house. Blinking, I looked again, sure I was dreaming. But the scene below didn't change.

Pounding footsteps raced up the stairs, and I didn't have time to react as Raven and Lexa ran into the room, shutting and locking the door. Seeing a shotgun in Raven's hands, I gulped and pressed myself back against the wall.

"What's going on?" I whispered.

"They found you," Lexa said, her voice steady as she looked out the window and then lifted it. "Hurry, this way."

I gaped at her as she climbed out and then reached back in to take my hand. When I didn't move fast enough, Raven nudged me. "Hurry, Tavia. We don't have much time."

Even as she was speaking, I heard more running feet, these much heavier. Quickly, I climbed through the window and out onto the roof. I'd barely gotten out when the bedroom door behind me was kicked in, and I heard two male voices speaking in rapid Russian.

"Tavia, this way!" Lexa yelled, climbing down from the roof. "Don't be scared. I'll help you."

But the sound of a gun firing had me screaming, and I looked back to find Raven standing by the open window, the gun pointed at one of the men who was approaching her. To my surprise, there was another man at her feet, blood pouring from where half his head had been blown off.

"Go!" Raven shouted.

The need to go back and help her was pushed aside at her command, and with Lexa's help, I jumped down just as I heard police sirens in the distance. Shattered glass, splintered wood, and house siding were all over the place, but Lexa didn't even seem bothered by it as she cushioned my drop. As soon as my feet were on the ground, she took hold of my wrist and we were running.

"Where?" I panted.

"Aunt Willa's," she said as we ran.

Less than a block later, a police cruiser skidded to a stop beside us. Ben jumped out, his eyes looking wild as he took in his wife. "I'm fine," she told him. "Mom is still back there. Hurry."

With a nod, he pulled his gun and took off at a dead run. Without missing a beat, Lexa tightened her hold on my wrist, and we were running again.

I didn't realize Willa lived so close until we ran up the steps of a two-story house several blocks away. Lexa didn't pause to knock, just turned the knob and pushed the front door open. "Aunt Willa! Safe room. Now."

"L-Lexa..."

We both froze in the living room at the sound of that soft, musical voice. Looking up, we both sucked in a gasp when we saw a huge man standing at the top of the stairs. His arm was around Monroe's waist, a gun pressed to her temple.

"Hello, niece," the man spat at me in a heavy accent.

I hadn't spent a lot of time analyzing Viktor Petrov's face the one and only time I'd met him, but right away, I could see the similarities between him and this man. The same wide nose. Same jawline. Same soulless eyes.

Out of instinct, I took a step back, but his hold on Monroe only seemed to tighten, making her whimper in pain and fright as he pressed the gun barrel harder into her temple. I froze, scared for the girl.

"Let her go," I told him, stepping forward and pulling my wrist free from Lexa's hold.

"Gladly," he said with a twist of his lips. "Once I have you."

"You won't get far," Lexa informed him, her tone chilled and baiting. "Even if you do leave here with Tavia, my husband won't let you past the end of the block."

Adas Petrov chuckled, the sound cold and evil. "Girl, you have no clue how capable I am of getting what I want. Your husband will only end up dead if he stands in my way."

"Lexa… Mom. Sh-she's…" Monroe cried out when Adas backhanded her to shut her up. The action sent her flying back on the stairs, her head hitting the step hard.

A sudden enraged roar behind us was all the warning we had that we weren't alone. A gun going off right beside my ear had Lexa and me dropping to the ground out of instinct. A pained grunt was followed by the heavy thud of Adas's body falling and then rolling down the stairs.

I felt more than heard the person behind me rush forward. They were so light on their feet, it was like they were a ghost. I lifted my head and saw a male dressed in all black, the hood of his sweatshirt pulled up over his head as he took the stairs three at a time. He bent, checking for a pulse on Monroe's neck. I heard him mutter something, but I couldn't understand what he was saying. It took me a few seconds to realize he was speaking Italian.

Then he was straightening and running past me again.

Lexa and I looked at each other, both of us too stunned by what had just happened to move for a moment. Then Monroe moaned, and we were both on our feet.

Lexa was faster than me and jumped over Adas's body before running up the stairs to reach her cousin. I moved to where my uncle was lying on the floor, the bullet wound in his chest gushing blood out onto the carpet as he gasped for breath.

I bent, looking into his eyes as the life slowly faded from him. I didn't even know this man, yet he wanted me dead. Right before my eyes, I watched him take his last breath, and I didn't feel a single ounce of remorse that he was dead.

"Monroe, who was that guy?" I heard Lexa demanding, pulling me back to what was going on around me.

"Don't tell anyone," the girl pleaded with a sob. "Daddy will kill him if he knows."

"Knows what?" Lexa half shouted. "A strange guy just killed a man for hitting you... Not that I'm complaining. He saved us all just now. But what the actual fuck, Monroe? You have some stalker with a hero complex or something?"

"Swear you won't tell anyone. Not even Ben," Monroe said in a voice that was growing stronger with each word. "Don't let them take him away from me."

"I don't understand any of this. But there's no time to discuss it. What's wrong with Aunt Willa?"

"That guy knocked her out in the kitchen then took me upstairs to wait for you."

I frowned down at them. "How did he know we would come here?"

Lexa's jaw tensed. "That, I don't know. Unless he has someone with insider intel. Which means we have a rat."

The pounding of feet on the porch alerted us to a new arrival. Ben came running in, sweat soaking his work shirt, both arms lifted with his gun at the ready. "Lexa?"

"I'm fine," she assured him. "Monroe might have a concussion, though. She hit her head and was out for a minute."

"Did you shoot this guy?" His brow was pinched. "You don't have a gun."

"I don't know who shot him," she told him honestly. "Someone came in behind us and shot him. I didn't see their face, and they were gone before I could get a look at them."

Walking over to the dead body, he kicked Adas in the ribs. "Well, it doesn't matter now. He's dead."

Things moved fast after that. More cops showed up, along with Raven and Monroe's father. The man they called Spider was the scariest motherfucker I'd ever seen with his head shaved and a tattoo of a deadly spider on his neck. He was taller than almost every man in the room, his shoulders even wider than Ben's. But it was the pure rage in his eyes that terrified me the most. Yet he was so gentle with Monroe that I was shocked speechless.

Lexa found Willa in the kitchen, still knocked out cold, and both Monroe and her mother were transported to the hospital by ambulance. Raven wrapped a blanket around me and made me sit on the couch in the living room while paramedics took Adas's body away.

The events of the evening were starting to catch up with me, and I shivered as reality began to set in. Adas was dead. Theo was gone. I was all alone. I didn't know what was going to happen to me next.

SIXTEEN

Yury was waiting for me at the airport when Anya's jet touched down. With Ivan out of commission from that bullet he took to the shoulder, it would just be Yury and me. Pops had worked out who all the traitors were within his men and had finally gotten Mom and Sofia's details sorted out, but they were still staying at Anya's home until I'd dealt with Petrov.

Without a word, I slid into the passenger seat of the SUV Yury was driving and picked up the Glock that was already waiting for me. I checked the clip then placed it in the holster under my jacket as he drove through the city.

I didn't expect Adas to be out in the open, enabling me to just pop him in the head a few times so I could to step back on the plane before the engines even had time to cool and I could return to Tavia. The bastard was too smart for that, especially after incurring Pops's wrath the night before when he'd attempted to have Sofia taken.

No, the motherfucker was probably in hiding, afraid for his life now that he was on Adrian Volkov's shit list.

But he would still want Tavia. His blood feud with the Bykov family was too strong for him to give up. I needed to be patient and set a trap to catch him before I could put a bullet in his brain.

And that meant letting everyone see me. If he knew I was back in the city, he would come straight for me. For one, because I'd killed his brother, but mostly because he knew I was hiding Tavia.

"Where to first, boss?" Yury asked.

It was early evening, but I could still make the first move.

"Let's make the rounds. I don't care where we start." All that mattered was that it would get me to the endgame.

Twenty minutes later, we were walking into one of the many clubs Pops was a silent partner in. I visited them all often, checking up on Pops's investments for him. The music was loud, and the liquor was flowing quickly.

Walking up the bar, I jerked my chin at the bartender, and he immediately set a glass of whiskey down in front of me. Lifting it, I tossed back the contents and motioned for another. This time, I picked up the glass and sipped as I turned to look around the club.

Across the room, Yury was standing guard, watching my back.

Pulling out my phone, I saw I had a few missed texts and grimaced.

Lexa: She doesn't want your presents. She's been in her room since this morning, from what Aunt Flick said. Didn't you tell her you were leaving, dumbass?

Me: I didn't want to worry her. Try again tomorrow with the presents.

Lexa: Fine, but I doubt she will accept them. You taking off without telling her, without so much as a 'goodbye,' is counterproductive to showing her you really do care about her, idiot. If you ask me…

Me: I didn't ask.

Lexa: If you ask me, your words seem pretty empty. Good luck proving to the woman you love her when all you do is show her she doesn't matter.

Muttering a curse, I tossed back the rest of the whiskey and motioned to the bartender for another. Lexa was right, but I couldn't worry about that yet. Once I knew Tavia was safe, I would deal with proving to her how much she meant to me.

"Hey, Theo."

I turned at the sound of my name to find a woman in a barely there dress walking toward me. Her long blond hair was curled over her shoulder, her lashes huge and fake, and I was positive those lips were just as surgically enhanced as her tits were. I couldn't remember her name, but I did remember her trying to seduce me the last time I was in this club.

I leaned back against the bar, watching her draw closer. I wasn't in the least bit interested, but the more people who saw me, the bigger the chance it would get back to Petrov. And there was no missing this woman.

Her hand slid up my chest as she stepped into my space, and I kept my face neutral to hide my revulsion. She wasn't my Tavia, and I hated her hands on me. Grasping her wrist, I pulled her off me.

"What do you want?" I asked her, my tone chilly and uninterested.

She pouted her thick lips up at me, the stark red of her lipstick and her barely there dress that left nothing to the imagination making her look like a porn star. She probably was for all I knew, but that kind of look did nothing for me. My cock only got hard for Tavia.

"It's been so long since I last saw you, lover," she purred, rubbing her free hand up my chest before snaking her arm around my neck. Leaning in, she inhaled deeply and moaned as if I'd just touched her clit. "Mm, you look delicious. Let's get out of here. I promise you won't regret it. Come on, baby. I'll ride your dick so good."

Disgusted with this bitch, I lifted her up and placed her on her feet away from me. "Pretty sure you come with a shot of penicillin. I'd rather not catch what you're carrying, honey." Her face turned blood red, and her mouth dropped open. She was so dumb, she was still trying to figure out if I'd just complimented or offended her.

Turning, I tossed a few bills on the bar top to cover my drinks before moving around the gape-mouthed hooker.

After three more clubs, I'd had enough, sure that at least someone would let Petrov know I was back.

I was tired and ready to call it a night, but instead of going to my apartment, I went to the compound to check on my sister since it wasn't too late.

The house where my aunt lived was so big, she and her husband and two kids lived there with Mom's twin sister, Scarlett, her husband, Ciro, and their five kids, with plenty of guest rooms to spare for when Nova and Garret came to visit during the summer. As soon as I stepped into the house, I was assaulted by pure chaos with Samara running around, dancing and playing.

Of all my cousins, she was the only one I was biologically connected to. She looked so much like Anya, especially her blue eyes, that it was almost like looking at a miniature version of my aunt.

"Theo. Theo. Theo!" Samara chanted my name when she spotted me. "Let's play."

I bent to lift her into my arms, her long dark hair falling over my wrists as I kissed her cheek. "Sorry, little one. I don't have time to play today."

Her bottom lip pouted out. "Maybe tomorrow?"

"We'll see," I said evasively and placed her back on her feet as Mom came into the room.

Her brown eyes lit up when she saw me, and I was instantly pulled in for a fierce hug. "How is Tavia?" she asked quietly, eyeing Samara for a moment to see if she repeated anything she said.

"She's healing," was all I could tell her, because the truth was, I didn't know how Tavia was doing at the moment. Lexa had said Tavia was in her room, and since she wouldn't take the things I'd sent Raven and Lexa to buy for her, I wasn't able to speak to her personally to know how she was feeling.

"And how has she been dealing with the loss of the baby?" Mom's dark eyes filled with sorrow. Because of how bad her diabetes was, she'd always been advised not to have children. She never seemed to let that bother her, though, having adopted first me and then Sofia when I was still a young boy.

I grimaced, unsure what to tell her. "She hasn't talked about it much, Mom. Maybe it's because of everything else going on, but she hasn't really dealt with the loss yet."

"Oh, that's not good, Theo. She needs to take time to grieve, or it's only going to get worse." She twisted her hands together, shaking her dark-red head. "Maybe I should fly out there and be with her. She needs a woman to help her through this right now."

"Raven is taking good care of her," I told her, giving her a quick kiss on the cheek. "But once I bring her home, you can take care of her all you want, Mom."

Light footsteps approaching had me lifting my head as Sofia walked into the room. When she saw me, her eyes lit up and then darkened when she glanced around and didn't see Tavia. "Where is she?" she demanded, crossing her arms over her chest. "What have you done with Tavia?"

"She's somewhere safe," was all I told her.

"You left her in some godforsaken safe house?" my sister seethed. "All alone with no one she knows to care for her while she's still recovering from being shot? How heartless can you be, you selfish bastard?"

"Sofia," Mom scolded. "You don't know anything about what is going on, so stop treating your brother like he's a douchebag."

Sofia snorted. "Could have fooled me."

"I didn't leave her alone. She's got people I trust watching over her. She's being well cared for, and she wants for nothing." When my sister only continued to glare at me, I threw up my hands. "Believe me or don't. I'm done discussing it with you. This is none of your business anyway."

"All right, that's enough," Mom snapped.

"No, Mom," Sofia said with a shake of her head. "It's not nearly enough. That's the whole problem. But I'm done discussing it too. So, don't worry, I won't bring it up again. After all, Theo is the one who is dicking around all over town, while the girl he should be taking care of is God only knows where."

"What is that supposed to mean?" I demanded, getting more pissed with my sister by the second.

She shoved her phone screen in my face. "Want to tell me why you're fucking around with Courtney Blanco while my best friend is still recovering from being shot?"

A picture of me lifting the blonde from earlier was in Sofia's social media feed. The picture had been taken just as I'd picked her up, so my hands were on her waist and she was lifted off her feet. If someone didn't know what happened next—that I'd put her away from me and walked off—they could easily assume the blonde had wrapped her legs around my waist.

"Nothing to say?" Sofia said with a humorless laugh. "I'm not surprised. You are such an asshole, Theo. Tavia deserves so much better than you."

Mom took the phone, her eyes narrowing when she saw the picture. "Theo... After all that poor girl has been put through recently, you do this? I thought I raised you better. I thought you were a better man than to—"

"Mom," I cut her off, my voice full of ice. "I only picked her up to get her away from me. I would never do something like that to Tavia."

"Sure you wouldn't," Sofia sneered. "You're like every other man on the planet, dear brother. Heartless and only thinking with your dick. Tavia is better off without you. I should have warned her off you when I first realized she had a crush on you. I can only blame myself, though."

"This picture is very damning, Theo." Mom shook her head sadly. "If Tavia were to see it, I'm sure it would cause her untold pain. Especially right now when she's so vulnerable."

A door slamming had us all turning. I grabbed my mom and sister, pushing them behind me, only then noticing that Samara was no longer in the room with us.

Pops stormed into the room, his face tense and gray. "We have a problem," he announced. "They found her."

Fuck. I never should have left her, not even for a second.

"I have to go," I muttered, already running for the door.

"Theo, be careful," Mom called after me. "Please, honey. Don't do anything reckless."

"Theo..." Sofia's pleading voice stopped me at the front door, and I turned impatiently to look at her. "Please, take care of Tavia...and yourself."

"I will, Sof. I promise."

SEVENTEEN

The night wore on, and it didn't seem like I was going anywhere anytime soon. I overheard Raven's brothers talking, saying that the structure of the house had to be checked out before anyone could go back in, but apparently they had a contractor who could do all of that the next morning.

I sat on the couch in a blanket Raven had wrapped around me, curled into a ball.

Thankfully, Flick had been gone to pick up Nova from a friend's house, and Garret had been next door when my uncle's henchmen had driven the van into the house. Raven and Lexa were both in the kitchen and not the living room, or things might have gone a hell of a lot differently.

No one said anything where I could hear them, but their strained, hushed whispers told me they were discussing me and who the rat Lexa had mentioned could be. All I could think was that I'd brought this evil into their lives. Because of me, Lexa and Raven could have been killed. Monroe and Willa, too.

All I brought with me were trouble and danger. No wonder no one cared about me.

Eventually, things began to quiet down, the blood-soaked carpet was rolled up and removed, and the cops left, along with Ben and Lexa. Mila came to sit with me and, soon after, her brother, Maverick. Mila turned on the television to some weird reality show I'd never heard of before, but apparently she couldn't not watch because Monroe had called her asking for cliff notes on the night's episode.

Max, Lexa's brother, joined us around nine, but by then, I was having trouble keeping my eyes open. My entire body ached, and I felt so tired, it was all I could do not to fall asleep sitting up. But I didn't know where I would be sleeping, and I didn't want to inconvenience anyone by asking for a bed on which to lie down. Especially when I'd caused so much trouble already.

More hours passed, more mindless TV watched, and I was trying in vain to stay awake.

But then I heard his voice, and everything inside me woke up instantly.

Turning my head, I looked over at the front door to find Theo walking into the house, five men I vaguely recognized as security for his family behind him. His face was tense, but when he saw me, it relaxed somewhat.

"Are you hurt?" he asked in a raspy voice.

I turned my gaze back to the television. "We both know you don't care, so why bother asking?"

"Tavia…" His voice was strained. "I'm sorry I wasn't here. I thought…" He trailed off, and I didn't care enough to know what he'd stopped himself from saying. "If you're uninjured, I would like to take you home."

That caught my attention. I jerked to my feet, grimacing when my muscles protested and locked for a moment before I turned to face him. "And just where is that? Huh? I don't have a home, Theo. I have a dorm room where I sleep and study. I don't have anything or anyone who cares if I live or die. So where exactly do you want to take me?"

"No one who cares if you live or die?" he repeated, his face darkening. "Everyone who meets you can't help but love you, krasotka. You are more precious to me than any other person in the world."

"Whatever. I'm not going to stand here and argue with you. Just take me back to New York so I can return to my classes." Folding the blanket I'd been huddled under all evening, I placed it on the couch beside Mila, who was watching Theo and me just as avidly as she'd watched her reality shows all night. "Please tell your sister and mom I'm so sorry for what happened. I hope they don't hate me too much for causing them so much trouble."

Mila stood, her warm hands clasping mine and squeezing. "None of this was your fault. I overheard Uncle Bash saying earlier they have a rat who must have been feeding that Petrov jerk-off intel. If they hadn't, no one would have even known you were here. So, this is on them, not you." She wrapped her arms around me, giving me a tight hug. "Don't be a stranger, Tavia. You were fun to hang out with, and I don't say that about just anyone. Monroe and I will both miss you."

I squeezed her back before turning and walking past Theo. But when I reached the door, his five goons stood in my way, blocking my exit.

Frustrated, I glared at Theo over my shoulder. "Well?"

Jaw clenching, he crossed to me. "Don't you want to say goodbye to Raven?"

No. I wanted to stay there with Raven forever. She'd taken such good care of me, made me feel like I mattered, and for a moment in time, I'd felt like I belonged somewhere. But I'd already caused her so much trouble. She'd had to shoot someone — maybe more than one someone — for me already. I didn't want to face her and see the condemnation in her green eyes.

Swallowing hard, I shook my head and pushed through the thugs in suits to walk outside. But instead of staying inside with Theo, they followed me out into the chilly early morning darkness. A huge SUV sat at the end of the driveway, and I knew right away it was Theo's.

Wrapping my arms around myself to fight off the cold, I walked toward it, keeping my head down because I was too ashamed to look at anyone.

"Tavia."

My shoulders tensed at the sound of Raven's voice. I stopped, but I couldn't make myself turn to look at her. Tears burned my eyes because I was going to miss her, but I couldn't continue to put her family at risk. Sure, Adas was dead, but did that mean no one else would want to kill me? Were there other people in the Petrov family who would want me dead?

Soft hands touched my bare arms as she turned me to face her. The streetlight cast her face in shadows, but I could still tell her eyes were narrowed. "You don't have to go, sweetheart. You're family now. Stay."

I lowered my lashes, trying to hide my tears, but one snuck out and ran down my cheek. "I can't," I whispered. "I've already put you and your wonderful family in enough danger as it is. Th-thank you for taking such good care of me. I... I'll never forget anything you did for me, Raven."

Her arms enfolded me in a warm hug, her hands stroking over my hair how I imagined a mother would her child's. "If you really want to go, I won't make you stay. But always remember that you have a place here with us if you ever need or want to come back. You're mine now, Tavia. I claimed you. That means you're a part of this family forever."

Two more tears fell, and I pressed my face into her shoulder. "Th-thank you so much," I choked out, trying to hold back a sob.

Pulling back, she stroked her thumb over my damp cheek. "I'm only a phone call away. If you need anything, don't hesitate. I'll pick up, no matter what time of day or night it is."

The lump in my throat wouldn't allow me to speak, so I nodded, and she smiled sadly. "Take care of yourself, sweetheart."

With another hug, she released me, and I made a dash to the waiting SUV before I completely broke down.

The five security guards stood outside the vehicle until Theo joined me a short time later. Once he was seated in the back with me, the others got in. Everyone remained quiet as we rode toward the airport. I kept my gaze trained on the window, unable to see anything but the passing lights, feeling as if my heart were breaking all over again with each mile that took me farther away from the family that had claimed me for so short a time.

EIGHTEEN

It was midafternoon before we made it back to New York. By then, I felt like I was in an all-new kind of hell.

Tavia had cried all the way to the airport, never once speaking to me, not even when I tried to talk to her. She wouldn't even look at me. Not that I could blame her. Somewhere over the Midwest, she fell asleep after fighting it for a few hours. But she stayed on the couch as far away from me as she could possibly be on the jet, sleeping curled into a little ball, as if trying to make herself as tiny as physically possible.

She was sound asleep when we touched down. Knowing I was risking making her even angrier with me, I carried her off the jet and to the waiting limo where Pops and my uncle Cristiano were waiting. Thankfully, she didn't stir and was still out cold by the time we reached my parents' house.

With Petrov now dead—something I was equal parts appreciative of and pissed over, because I'd wanted to be the one to put a bullet in the bastard's skull just as I'd done his brother—there was no reason for Mom and Sofia to stay at Anya's any longer.

Pops watched Tavia with concerned eyes as we rode toward the compound where I'd grown up. "She looks fragile," he murmured quietly.

"I know." Pushing a few locks of hair back from her face, I ached to kiss her but didn't want to chance waking her before I got her home to Mom.

I didn't need her to tell me she wasn't going to let me take care of her, but I was hoping Mom could get her to at least let her take over the care Raven had been giving her. Anything was better than her going back to her dorm, where no one would be able to make sure she was okay. Maybe Mom and Sofia could help her heal in more than just the physical sense.

My fuckups with her seemed unending, and I honestly didn't know how to make it all right, but I was going to try my damnedest.

When the limo rolled to a stop in front of my childhood home, I got out and carefully reached back in to lift Tavia into my arms. With a sigh, she wrapped her arms trustingly around my neck.

At least in her sleep she knew she could trust me. Too bad I hadn't proved it to her to make her understand that when she was conscious.

But she would.

Mom was already standing at the door when I walked up the front steps. As I entered the house with Dad and Uncle Cristiano behind us, Sofia came running down the stairs. A look from Dad had her clamping her mouth closed before she could say anything that might wake up the precious cargo in my arms.

Taking one look at Tavia's paleness, Mom led the way up to one of the guest rooms she'd already prepared for Tavia's arrival. Once I placed her in the middle of the bed, I stepped back, but I didn't exit the room as I was sure Sofia expected me to since she was standing guard at the foot of the bed.

Mom tucked the covers up over Tavia, who didn't even move once her head was on one of the plush pillows. "I've already spoken to Raven Reid. She told me all about Tavia's diet." Her brown eyes turned on me. "Among other things."

I clenched my jaw, making the muscles tick. "I honestly thought I was doing the right thing leaving her there while I tried to draw out Petrov. She was supposed to be safe in California."

"I'm not the one you need to explain yourself to, Theo," she said with a pained exhale. "Right now, I think you should go and let Tavia get some rest. You look like you could use some sleep yourself. Go on. I'll tend to her. She will be completely fine in my care."

My gaze lingered on Tavia's sleeping face. There were circles under her eyes so dark, they looked like bruises marring her delicate skin. The woman I loved was inches away from breaking, and it was my fault.

"Get out, Theo," Sofia hissed.

"I've about had it with your shit, Sof," I gritted out, but after one more lingering look down at Tavia, I forced myself to walk to the door.

When I opened the door, it was to find Pops standing there with not only my uncle, but my cousin Ryan as well. The young teen stood there looking bored, his arms crossed over his chest.

"What?" I said with a grunt, only wanting to get to bed for a few hours of sleep before going back to Tavia.

"There isn't a rat in the MC," Pops announced.

"How do you know?"

Cristiano nodded his head toward the stairs. "Let's take this conversation downstairs."

I followed the three of them to Pops's office at the back of the house on the first floor. As soon as the door closed behind me, I was demanding answers.

"Mom told me about what happened last night when I got home from school," Ryan informed me. "When she said that the guy set up a trap and lured Tavia to Nova's Uncle Spider's house, I realized someone must have been listening in to our conversations. Two days ago, I asked Nova what she would do if someone ever attacked her at her house and she was alone. I was worried about her with Tavia there and all the heat I've been hearing Pop and Mom talking about lately."

"And she told you the protocol? The safe room in Masterson's house they're supposed to stay in until help arrives?" Ryan nodded, and I stabbed my fingers through my hair in frustration before turning to Pops and Cristiano. "Who the fuck is listening in to your conversations?"

"Last week, someone at ball practice asked to use my phone because his died and he didn't have a charger with him. He said he was calling his mom to make sure she knew when to pick him up after practice. I barely talk to the guy, but I didn't think anything of it." Ryan grimaced. "I should have known better, and I'm sorry. My ignorance put everyone in danger, including Nova."

Cristiano put a hand on his son's shoulder. "We know you didn't mean for this to happen, Ryan. You have to be more careful in the future, though. Understand?"

"Yeah, Pop." His brown eyes met mine. "I'm sorry, Theo."

"It's not like you did it on purpose, dude. You had no idea what was going on, and if you had, I know you wouldn't have let it happen. Especially where Nova is concerned." I looked at Pops and my uncle. "Does the MC know?"

"Ciro called Hannigan after Ryan told Anya what he thought happened. His man, Desi, is looking at the chip on the phone now. We will hopefully know more soon." Cristiano nodded his head at the door. "We're headed home, but I'll let you both know more when I have the details."

I watched them go then turned back to Pops. "With Petrov dead, is there anyone who would want to harm Tavia?"

"I'm looking into that too, son. But Viktor and Adas were the last of the Petrov line that I know of. With them both gone..." His brow furrowed. "You realize Tavia will inherit everything from both the Petrov and Bykov families, right? If you step in and take over the Petrov territories, manage everything for her, she will never want for anything."

"She would never want for anything anyway, Pops. I'll always make sure of that."

NINETEEN

Waking up in strange beds seemed to be my new norm. As I opened my eyes, I wasn't even surprised to find I was in a new room in a new house.

Having Theo's mom standing at the foot of the bed smiling down at me, however, was a shock. I clenched my fingers in the soft material of the covers and quickly sat up, glancing around to try to figure out what time it was.

The thick drapes over the windows didn't give a clue, but there was a digital clock on the nightstand that told me it was just after eight in the evening.

"I was starting to worry about you." She picked up her phone, texting quickly. "Are you hungry?

Thirsty? I've had our cook on standby for when you wake up. What would you like to eat?"

"I…" I frowned, unsure of how I was feeling just yet, as sleep still clouded my mind. I didn't feel hungry, and while my mouth was parched, I wasn't sure I wanted something to drink either.

More than anything, I just wanted to go back to my dorm and hide from Mrs. Volkov and the rest of the world.

"You're probably feeling sticky after that long flight and the excitement of last night. Why don't you take a shower while I go down and put you a tray together?" She lifted her gaze to mine and smiled again. "All of your things have already been put away, but if you can't find something, just let me or Sofia know."

"My…things?" I repeated, confused.

"Your clothes, toiletries, books, and everything else. I had Adrian go to your dorm and pack up all of your things since you will be staying here with us from now on."

"What?" I pushed back the covers and started to stand, but Mrs. Volkov rushed around and pressed me back down with a firm hand.

"Easy, sweetheart. I don't want you to hurt yourself moving around too quickly. You're just starting to really heal."

"I'm fine," I gritted out, more than a little frustrated with her. "Mrs. Volkov, I can't stay here. I don't want to be a bother, and I'd much rather be in my dorm. Honestly, I'm better now, and I don't need a nurse or a babysitter or—"

"Tavia, sweetheart, you're staying here because you are dear to us, and I won't have you all alone in that cold and lonely dorm with no one to care for you if you become ill." She tenderly brushed my hair back from my face. "You are like one of my children. I care for you very much. Now, don't argue. There's no use in it anyway. I always get my way." With a wink, she stepped back. "Now, you take that shower. I'll be right back."

Feeling like I'd just been hit by a whirlwind, I sat there gaping after the woman for several minutes. Finally shaking my head, I focused on getting up and doing as she suggested.

As she said, my toiletries were all in the bathroom, including a box of tampons. For some reason, I laughed at the sight of them, picturing Sofia's dad packing up my bathroom and touching the very feminine box. Her dad was more than a little intimidating, so it amused me to think of him flushing pink while he handled my hygiene items.

Yet I knew he would have done it without complaint if his wife was the one who had asked him to. That was one thing I'd never wondered about when it came to the Volkovs. That man loved his wife so much, I didn't question him jumping to do his wife's bidding for the smallest of tasks.

The bathroom was gigantic with the toilet hidden behind a partial wall and a long vanity where even my toothbrush was waiting. The doors of the shower were a beautiful stained glass and the shower heads powerful enough to unknot the tightest of muscles. It was big enough for three people to stand in and still have room to move around easily. There was a clawfoot tub adjacent to the shower that I ached to sink into and soak for hours, but I couldn't submerge myself until the medical tape over the incisions on my abdomen completely faded.

I took my time showering, the jets making me moan helplessly in pure nirvana. When I stepped out a long while later, there was a towel hanging beside the shower door along with a plush robe, and I realized Mrs. Volkov must have come in without my noticing.

I dried then wrapped the towel around my hair before putting on the robe. It was so soft and thick, I sighed with contentment, but I quickly told myself not to get used to this kind of luxury. I wasn't going to be staying long, just until I could convince Mrs. Volkov I would be fine on my own, and then I would go back to the dorm.

Opening the bathroom door, I took two steps into the bedroom, only to stop in my tracks. It wasn't Mrs. Volkov standing in the middle of the room with a tray, but her son.

Had he been the one to leave the robe and towel? Had he seen me, yet again, in the shower? I didn't know, wasn't about to ask, and was suddenly very thankful for the beautiful stained glass of the shower stall that had hidden my body from him.

He turned to face me as I walked farther into the room, his eyes unreadable as he watched me take a step closer to the bed. But closer to the bed meant closer to him, and I paused, unsure how far I could get before I completely broke down at his nearness.

"Mom had to take a call, so she sent me with food," he murmured in that deep voice that stupidly still had the power to make me shiver.

I wrapped my arms around myself, trying to hide in the robe. From him. From the world. But more than anything, from myself and the confusing feelings he could still produce in me even after all the pain and gut-wrenching heartache he'd caused me—was still causing.

When I just stood there, unmoving, unspeaking, he pressed his lips into a hard line. "Is this how it's going to be now, krasotka? You not even speaking to me, and me aching for just a smile from you?"

"What do you want from me, Theo?" I asked in a voice raspy with emotion and disuse. "I have nothing. Am nothing. I don't understand what you could possibly want from me."

"You," he said. "Only you."

"I don't believe you," I whispered, and a flash of pain crossed his face.

"I know. You don't trust me, and I can't blame you. I've done nothing to show you how I feel. Given you no reason to believe a word that leaves my mouth. But you will. I'll prove it all to you, make you believe in me and what I feel for you."

I stood there, looking up at him, skeptically thinking he was totally full of shit. He had a way with words, that was for sure. If I hadn't known him so well, I might have thought he was sincere. But unfortunately for him, I knew his words had absolutely zero value to them.

How many times had he made me think he cared, only to leave me without so much as a word? How many times since I was shot had he said he loved me, only to back it up with nothing at all?

I was tired of everything. This game he was playing was probably fun for him. But for me, it was exhausting, and I had no more energy to spare. It was all I could do just to lift my head and stay upright in front of him, when all I really wanted to do was curl into a ball and stay that way until the life finally faded from my soul.

Two taps on the bedroom door alerted us to a newcomer just as it opened and Sofia stuck her dark head into the room. When she saw me standing there, her face split into a beaming smile, and she rushed toward me.

I was engulfed in her tight hug. "I'm so glad you're awake. I've been so worried about you." She leaned back, her blue eyes finding mine. "How are you feeling? Still tired? In pain? Hungry?"

"I have her tray right here, Sof," Theo informed her, and Sofia's gaze snapped to him, her eyes darkening as they took him in.

Stepping back, she crossed the distance to her brother and took the tray from his hands. "How kind of you. Now get out."

Guardedly, I watched the two siblings. After witnessing their tight-knit relationship over the years, seeing the tension between them now was a bit surreal. Yet animosity was flowing off Sofia like a physical entity. It was so powerful, it felt as if her rage could slash through her brother like barbed wire.

Yet as confused as I was by this new strain between the two of them, I was glad to have her pushing him out the door.

"I'm staying," Theo informed her.

"Stay in the house all you want," his sister told him tightly. "But you have no reason to be in Tavia's room. She's no longer your responsibility, and from the way she's cowering from you right now, it's safe to say that your company is at the bottom of her list."

"She and I need to talk," he told her in a menacing tone. "You're the one who needs to get out."

"I seriously doubt there is anything the two of you have to talk about. You did your part. She's back where she belongs, where Mom and I can take care of her. Now, you should just leave her in peace and allow her to heal. Seeing as though all of this is your fault to begin with." Walking around him, she set the tray on the end of the bed. When she straightened, her bright smile was back in place. "Come. You must be starving. You can tell me all about your time in California while you eat."

Food wasn't at the top of my priority list, nor was telling her about my stay on the other side of the country. But more than anything, I didn't want to have to pass Theo to get to the bed.

"Krasotka, please don't send me away," he pleaded quietly, taking a step toward me.

On instinct, I took two steps back, lowering my gaze to the floor.

"Do you call everyone 'krasotka,' brother dear?" Sofia's voice was like the sharp lash of a whip. "Did you call Courtney Blanco that last night when you were holding her in the club?"

Another slice of pain struck me in the center of my chest. I had no idea who Courtney Blanco was, but the pure conviction I heard in my friend's voice told me she wasn't just standing there making up hypothetical questions for him. Whoever the woman was Sofia was talking about, Theo had been with her. The night before. Only hours after leaving me behind in California. Alone.

I'd never thought about him calling anyone else besides me "krasotka." It was a beautiful endearment, one that sounded both passionate and loving when he spoke it. I thought if nothing else, it meant I was a little special to Theo.

But I really should have known better.

TWENTY

Right before my eyes, what little fight I'd seen in Tavia's eyes faded like a dying candle. Seeing the light completely disappear left me cold.

Fuck this shit. I was tired of Sofia running her mouth when she didn't know the first thing she was talking about. She had no clue about my life, even though she wanted to think she was an expert on all things Theo.

Picking up my sister by the waist, I carried her to the door.

"What the hell are you doing?" she screeched, thrashing her legs and trying to make me drop her. "Theo! Put me down. Put. Me. Down!"

I placed her on the other side of the threshold before slamming the door in her face and flipping the lock. She pounded on the door with her fists, her voice full of rage as she demanded to be allowed inside.

Ignoring her, I went back to Tavia, who was watching me with a neutral expression on her beautiful face, and lifted her into my arms. She felt even lighter than normal as I carried her to bed and placed her so her back was against the pillows.

Turning her head away, she tried to hide from me, but I was done with all of this bullshit. Taking her chin between my thumb and forefinger, I leaned over her and forced her to look at me. "I returned to New York yesterday and went straight to the clubs my father is a silent partner in. Three of them, in fact."

She looked at me blankly with her darker-than-espresso eyes, but I continued my explanation. "My plan was to draw Petrov's attention, make him come out of hiding so I could set a trap and catch him. I wanted to protect you, and that meant eliminating the bastard. Courtney was at the club, she came on to me, and I picked her up and set her away from me, like I just did with Sofia. But someone took a picture and posted it to social media. It was taken at the perfect time because it looked as if things were going to happen, but the truth is, I put that skank as far from me as I could, and I got the fuck out of there."

"Why are you telling me this?" Her voice was devoid of all emotion, as blank as her eyes were, and I fucking hated it.

"Because you deserve to know why I left. And my sister thinks she knows everything, but she doesn't know shit. I didn't leave you behind, Tavia. I came back here to protect you. And as soon as I took out Petrov, I was going to return for you."

"You're good at leaving, Theo. It's all you've ever done with me. I don't expect anything less." Jerking her head back, she made me drop my hold on her chin and scooted over several inches, putting space between us. "I'm tired. Anything you feel you have to say or explain, save your breath. I don't want to hear any of it."

"Too fucking bad. I'm not leaving here until you understand everything." Reaching down to the foot of the bed, I picked up the tray and placed it across her lap. "Eat."

"I'm not hungry," she said in a small voice.

"Eat, or I will feed you, krasotka," I threatened, only to see her flinch. Biting back a curse, I cupped her face in one hand. Fucking Sofia and her big-ass mouth. All she'd wanted to do was score points off me, yet all she'd accomplished was hurting Tavia more. "You are the only one I have ever used that endearment for. Fuck, you're the only woman I have ever used any endearment for at all. No one else matters enough to me. Only you, Tavia. Only ever you."

She lowered her lashes, hiding her eyes from me. "Your charm is award-winning, Theo. Too bad I see through it."

My heart sank, realizing that even though I was telling her what was in my heart, she didn't believe me. Not that I could blame her, but fuck, I needed her to trust me, if only just a little. If there was none left for her to give me, how could I win her back?

"Baby, you mean everything to me—"

"Obviously," she said in that same toneless voice that sent chills down my spine.

"I know I've made mistakes, but you are the only one in my heart. Give me a chance to show you that above everything else. All I want is to make you happy." Clutching her hands in both of mine, I begged her with my eyes, but the look in her dark depths never changed. It was like there was nothing there, as if her soul was just...gone.

"Listen to me, Tavia," I commanded, desperation deepening my voice. "I will never leave you again. I'm going to spend the rest of our lives showing you how much I love you, how much you mean to me. If it takes me until my dying day to prove it to you, I don't care."

"Sure," she said with a nod. "Okay. Yeah. Whatever you say, Theo."

The lack of belief in her voice wounded me, but again, it wasn't anything I didn't deserve. Fighting back the frustration of being unable to get through to her, I sat on the edge of the bed and picked up the bowl of overcooked bowtie pasta and creamy white sauce. There were peas mixed in to the dish, and I took the fork off the tray.

Lifting a bite, I touched it to her closed lips. "Eat for me," I insisted.

She shook her head. "I'm not hungry."

"You haven't eaten in over twenty-four hours. You need food to get your strength back. Raven gave Mom plenty of meal ideas to keep you happy while still following the soft food diet the doctors said was necessary while your intestines heal." I teased her bottom lip with the fork. The food smelled good even if it didn't look overly appealing to me. I'd already had dinner with Pops, and it had been a hell of a lot more fulfilling than this seemed.

Some of the cream sauce smeared across her full bottom lip, and she snuck out her tongue to swipe it clean. Once she tasted it, her eyes drifted closed, enjoying the flavors. It was the first real sign of emotion I'd seen from her since Sofia had started running her mouth, and I felt something untwist in my chest.

Smiling at her in approval, I touched the fork to her lips again, and this time, she opened up just enough for me to slide the food inside. As she chewed, I glanced over the rest of the items on the tray. A cup of the ice cream the cook was famous for. It was sugar-free so Mom was able to eat it, but it sure as hell didn't taste like it was lacking the good stuff. Tavia had always loved this dessert, so I knew she wouldn't be able to turn it down.

For the next few minutes, she allowed me to feed her, but then she spotted the dish of ice cream, and I knew the pasta would no longer hold any appeal. I started to pick it up, wanting to continue to take care of her like this, but she snatched it from my hand and grabbed the spoon, digging in with a contented sigh.

Grinning at how childlike she was acting, I placed the tray on the nightstand and then reached for the remote to the television. With the push of a button, the TV came to life, and I sat back against the pillows beside her and channel-surfed while she enjoyed her dessert.

"I like this show," she said around the spoon still in her mouth then pointed it toward the TV set. "I didn't think I would like that guy as this character, but he's actually my favorite now."

"I've never watched it." Her eyes were glued to the television, but mine were on her, watching her eyes follow the characters on the screen while taking random bites of her ice cream.

Fuck, she was so damn beautiful.

"What?" she grumbled when she caught me staring. "Do I have ice cream on my face?"

"Yeah," I lied and leaned in, kissing her bottom lip. The cool, sweet honey of her mouth hit my taste buds, and I couldn't hold back a groan. My hand caught the back of her head, holding her in place so

I could deepen the kiss and suck on that luscious bottom lip.

With a soft gasp, she pulled back, her eyes narrowing on me. "I…I don't think this is a good idea. I'm not supposed to… To…"

I stroked my thumb over her cheek. "It's just a kiss, krasotka. That's all I want for now. I promise you, I won't ever do anything you don't say you want." Brushing her damp hair back from her face, I wrapped my arm around her and tucked her head against my shoulder.

When she didn't struggle or pull away, I took that as a small victory and kissed the top of her head. Small steps, I told myself. Small, delicate steps were what I needed to take to prove to her that I meant every word I said.

TWENTY-ONE

Sofia sighed and shifted restlessly on the bed beside me, her homework spread out in front of both of us. When she did it again, for the tenth time, I dropped my pencil and frowned at her.

"What's wrong with you?" I asked, more than a little irritated, but it wasn't all her fault.

I was restless too. Over the past two weeks, Mrs. Volkov had continued to insist I stay in bed as much as possible. She or Theo brought me my meals. They kept me company throughout the day when Sofia was at school, but I was going stir-crazy locked in the guest room. If I so much as walked downstairs,

Theo picked me up and carried me right back to my room.

But at least he stayed once he placed me in bed. Most of the time, he would call down to the kitchen to order us a snack and then climb into bed beside me so we could binge-watch something on Netflix.

He never tried to kiss me, but he would wrap his arms around my waist and stroke my hair until my head felt weak. Then I would pillow it on his shoulder and fall asleep right there in his arms.

To say I was conflicted where he was concerned would have been the biggest understatement of my entire life. He confused the hell out of me, and I didn't know what to make of this change in him. Sure, he'd said he was going to prove how much I meant to him, that he loved me, but I still wasn't sure if I believed him or not.

Part of me wanted him to be sincere, but a bigger part of me kept waiting for his real motives to make themselves known. It was like I was holding my breath, waiting—always waiting—for him to show me what a joke he really thought I was.

"Sorry," Sofia said with a grimace. "I'm just bored as hell. I haven't gotten to go anywhere outside of school or my cousins' house in almost a month. I'm starting to get cabin fever, and it's making me twitchy."

"Trust me, I know what you're feeling," I told her with a twist of my lips. At least she'd gotten to go to school, though, and to visit with her family. With Raven, I'd been allowed outside a little to soak up the sunshine and breathe the fresh air. But Theo refused to even talk about me going back to class yet, saying I was still too weak. At least he'd arranged with all my professors to finish out the semester online and made sure my scholarship wasn't jeopardized.

Sofia must have been thinking something sly, because a devious grin tilted at her lips. "Let's sneak out," she said, lowering her voice as if she thought someone was listening at the door. "Go to a club or something. Have some fun. We deserve a break from all this schoolwork bullshit, and you seem perfectly fine to me. I don't know what Theo and Mom are so worried about."

Neither did I. There was no soreness left, the doctor had let me graduate from soft foods to a normal diet, and had even encouraged me to do more physical activity. Yet the Volkovs treated me like I was delicate glass that would shatter under the slightest pressure.

It was maddening.

And sweet. So fucking sweet.

Which only drove me crazy because the sweetness of it made it impossible for me to stay mad at either Theo or his mom when it came to their bossiness about staying in bed and taking it easy.

But Sofia's whispered suggestion held great appeal. I bit my lip, glancing at the door, then my closet. "I don't have anything to wear," I whispered.

"Please," she said with a snort. "I have plenty for you to choose from. So, we doing this or what?"

Before I could talk myself out of it, I nodded.

She bounced up to her knees. "Yay! You shower, and I'll be back with a few things for you to pick from." Hopping off the bed, she headed for the door. "Good thing Theo is in meetings all evening. That makes sneaking out so much easier."

I rushed through a shower and then did my hair. I didn't have much experience with makeup since it had always been out of my budget, but when Sofia returned, she had a bag full of things I didn't even understand how to apply. Within an hour of her suggesting we go out, I was looking in the mirror at a complete stranger.

My friend had a gift, that was for freaking sure. I didn't even recognize myself with the way she'd highlighted certain parts of my face, while making other areas seem like they weren't even there. The outfit I'd picked from the pile of clothes she'd brought was a simple sleeveless black dress. There was no back to it, but there was a built-in bra so my boobs weren't bare. The hem ended a few inches short of midthigh, and the heels Sofia insisted looked amazing with it were gold and six inches high.

How the hell I was going to sneak out of the house—which was basically a damn fortress—in those neckbreakers I wasn't sure, but Sofia didn't seem all that concerned about it.

It was another hour later—and a few heart-stopping moments when I was sure we were going to be eaten by the dogs that roamed the Volkovs' property—that we walked into a club in the middle of downtown.

Sofia at my side, we'd been ushered straight inside, bypassing the line and the hundred or so people standing on the sidewalk outside of Project X.

There were two levels to the club, and after taking my hand, Sofia led me to the second floor. A bouncer at the bottom of the stairs gave her a lifted brow but stepped aside without question. At the top of the stairs, a hostess-like person was already waiting.

"Welcome, Miss Volkov," the woman greeted, her smile bright, but something in her eyes suggested she was nervous. "How long will you and your friend be joining us tonight?"

"As long as we fucking want," Sofia told her. "We're going to be in that back corner. Keep the drinks coming, and keep the goons away because we're here to have fun, not have your trained apes chase all the guys away."

The woman pressed her lips into a firm line but nodded. "As you wish, Miss Volkov."

Without another look at the hostess, Sofia pulled me through the crowd to the corner she had indicated, and we plopped down on a long, buttery-soft couch. No sooner had our butts touched the seats than there was a waitress asking for our drink orders.

After ordering for both of us, Sofia waved the girl away and then let her eyes trail over the people in our vicinity. I was doing a little people watching myself. This was the first time I'd been to this club. Really, it was my first trip to any club. I was always too busy with school and tutoring to even think about partying, so this was all a new experience for me.

The music was loud, but not so much that we had to yell to be heard when we spoke to each other. The lights were dim, giving the whole place an intimate ambiance. There was no mistaking that the people on this floor all came from money. Every single one of the women had on jewelry that looked like it could easily fund small countries. But it wasn't so much what they were wearing as how they held themselves that told me all of these people were used to snapping their fingers and getting what they wanted then and there.

Our drinks arrived, both of them nonalcoholic since Sofia wasn't flashing her fake ID around. I sipped at my cola and listened to Sofia as she filled me in on several people and the juicy details of their social lives. I didn't know how she kept up with all the things going on in other people's lives and still remembered all the stuff she needed to in order to pass her classes. But some of the stories she told me were so amusing, I was almost in tears from laughing so hard.

It felt good to be out of the house, out from under Theo's and Mrs. Volkov's watchful eyes and to just breathe. I didn't have to wonder what Theo's motives were for spending time with me or worry about hurting his mother's feelings if I did or said something unknowingly wrong.

There was just Sofia and me and the music and a club full of strangers who didn't know me from Eve. It was so easy to let my guard down.

Two guys in dress slacks and button-down shirts took a seat across from us. I let my eyes skim over them both. The one in the blue shirt had pretty green eyes, while the one in black had on glasses that were tinted ever so slightly to restrict his exposure to the strobes on the dance floor below. They were both leanly muscular, and going off the identical shape of their jaws, I was sure they were brothers or at least cousins.

Sofia smiled at the one in the blue shirt, and the guys both asked if they could buy us drinks. She was quick to accept, but this time, instead of nonalcoholic beverages, she told them we wanted shots.

The guy ordered a bottle of vodka and a bottle of tequila from the waitress. Both drinks were quickly brought back and set on the low table that separated our seats from theirs, along with four shot glasses.

I'd never had liquor before, and I wasn't exactly keen to try it now, but I didn't want to be the odd one out. Promising myself I'd only have one shot from each bottle, I tipped the vodka to my lips and downed the drink just as Sofia did.

But no sooner had our glasses touched the table than the guy wearing the glasses filled them back up.

My throat was on fire from the first shot, so I wasn't about to down another so quickly. Pushing it away, I sat back, sipping at the drink Sofia had ordered for me earlier in the hope that my throat would stop burning soon.

Sofia, however, was already on her third shot. I didn't know how well she could handle her liquor, so I watched her closely. One thing I noticed instantly was she got more and more flirty with each shot she took, and soon she was sitting on the other couch with the guy in blue.

Which meant the guy in black moved to sit beside me.

He sat down, his thigh brushing against mine, and gave me a smug little grin. "I'm AJ," he said, offering me his hand.

"Tavia," I muttered, placing mine in his just to be friendly.

His fingers tightened when I started to pull away, his thumb skimming over the backs of my knuckles for a moment. I frowned down at our joined hands and couldn't help thinking of when Theo did that exact same thing. Only when Theo did it, butterfly wings started to stir in my stomach. With AJ, all I felt was annoyance.

"Pretty name. But I expected nothing less from a woman so beautiful."

I barely stopped myself from rolling my eyes. If that wasn't a line he used on every woman, I didn't know what was.

Time passed slowly as Sofia flirted and got closer and closer to the guy in blue, while I sat there barely paying attention to AJ. I laughed when it seemed like that was what he expected, nodded from time to time, and made the appropriate noises as he told me his life story and tried to get me to do another shot.

"The fuck are you doing sitting beside my woman?" a voice full of savage menace demanded, and I snapped my head up to find Theo only feet away.

Dressed in a suit that looked like it had been painted onto his body, it fit him so damn well, he stood behind Sofia's couch, but his dark eyes were on AJ and me. More specifically, on how close AJ was sitting to me, his thigh practically molded to mine.

Theo didn't even seem to notice his sister was right in front of him, more on the guy's lap beside her than on the actual couch. I didn't know how he knew we were there, but I was happy to see him.

For one, I was bored talking to AJ. He wasn't fun at all, and every word out of his mouth was a well-rehearsed act to get into my pants. For another, I'd been kind of...sort of...missing Theo.

More than a little.

Maybe even a lot.

TWENTY-TWO

One minute I was walking across the second floor of Project X, about to go into a meeting with the general manager who had worked there for ten years under Adas Petrov's rule. And the next, I spotted Tavia sitting on a couch in a back corner, some douchebag practically on her lap, looking at her hungrily.

For the past two weeks, I'd been handling the changeover from Adas as the head of the Petrov businesses to putting everything in order for Tavia. Finding her in the same club she was now the sole owner of, thanks to Pops and me securing her inheritance, was not the kind of surprise I welcomed.

She should have been home in bed, resting and doing the homework she needed to catch up on.

Taking it easy. Waiting for me to come home and climb into bed beside her for our nightly cuddles and binge-fest.

It was the best part of my day, getting to wrap my arms around her, inhale the sweet scent of her shampoo, feel her warmth seep into me, and know she was safe. And mine.

Very, very much mine.

Something the douchebag beside her apparently didn't know, or he wouldn't have been within ten feet of my Tavia.

Jealousy and rage had me around the couch and jerking the fucker up by his shirt collar. He let out a startled yelp. "Hey, man. What's your problem?" he snarled, trying to push me back.

I pulled him closer, getting in his face. "Who said you could sit beside my woman?" I demanded. "Who gave you permission to touch what is mine?"

"Hey, hey, hold up. She's not your property." When he couldn't push me away, he covered my fists balled around the material of his shirt with his hands. "Dude, let me go. I don't want to hurt you."

"Theo." Tavia was on her feet, trying to push her way between me us. "Theo, calm down. We were just talking. Nothing was happening."

"Don't give a fuck." Releasing one of my hands from the hold on his shirt, I swept her behind me, out of the line of fire, shielding her with my body while still easily holding on to the guy in front of me. "You ever come near what is mine again, and you'll be eating teeth. You fucking get me, dude?"

"Dude, I'm serious. I'm about to kick your goddamn ass if you don't let me go."

I lifted my brows at him in challenge, daring him to even try.

He muttered something under his breath and swung at me. But I was faster. Releasing him, I blocked his punch then landed one of my own straight to his sternum. He bent in half with a groan, and I pushed him back onto the couch he'd just been sharing with Tavia. "Stay the fuck away from her," I repeated.

Turning, I cupped her shocked face in both my hands and lowered my head to brush my lips over her gaping mouth. The taste of her on my tongue, the feel of her under my fingertips, calmed me a little, so when I pulled back, my voice wasn't nearly as harsh when I spoke. "You should be in bed."

"I—We were bored. Really, Theo, you can't expect me to stay locked up forever. I'm fine now."

"Maybe you are physically, but emotionally, you aren't even close to being fine." I tucked a few strands of her hair behind her ear and skimmed my thumb down her neck. "Once you've learned to cope with the grief of losing the baby, then we can discuss you going out. But only if I'm available to go with you, krasotka."

Tears instantly filled her eyes. "That...That's the first time you've even mentioned the baby since you told me about the miscarriage," she murmured, and I realized she was right.

Fuck. How could I expect her to just recover from the loss when I wasn't even trying to help her deal with it?

Swallowing hard, I kissed her again. "Let's go home, yeah?"

Blinking back her tears, she gave a small nod, and I kissed her one more time before turning and grabbing my sister. She was half straddling some guy's lap, completely clueless as to what was going on around her. When I picked her up and set her on her feet beside me, she cursed me. But I didn't even give her time to throw a tantrum as I linked my fingers through Tavia's and then wrapped my free hand around Sofia's upper arm.

The trip home was anything but pleasant with Sofia drunkenly calling me every name she could think of in three different languages. She got more creative with her Italian than her Russian, but it was what she called me in English that had Tavia turning pink and keeping her face hidden behind her hair as I ignored my sister's tirade of inventive curse words from the back seat.

Our parents were out for the evening, which was probably for the best. I slung Sofia over my shoulder and carried her up to her room after texting Yury and telling him I needed him to stand guard at my sister's bedroom door to make sure she didn't try to sneak out again that night.

When she was settled, I went to Tavia's room, where she'd said she was going once we walked through the front door. She had already changed into pajama pants and a baggy T-shirt, her hair up in a messy knot on top of her head and her face washed clean of makeup.

She'd looked good earlier in her club clothes and makeup, but fuck, I loved her all-natural more. Her face was so much more beautiful without all that shit.

Almost shyly, she looked up at me through her lashes. "Everything okay?" she asked softly as she shifted to the middle of the bed to make room for me, the remote already in one hand.

"She's drunk and feisty, so a typical Friday night for Sofia. Only, it's Thursday." Kicking off my shoes, I tossed my suit jacket on the chair near the window and then climbed in beside Tavia.

But when I took the remote she offered, I placed it on the nightstand and reached for her instead. I wrapped my hand around her neck, my thumb tilting up her chin so I could kiss her at the perfect angle. A soft sigh escaped her, and she opened her mouth, letting me inside without a fight.

At the first taste of her on my tongue, my cock began to throb, but I kept the kiss slow, not deepening it at all even when she squirmed against me, silently asking for more. My hands didn't explore her amazing body like I wanted to. It was just me and Tavia and this kiss.

When I finally released her mouth, she was breathing hard, her chest rising and falling rapidly as if she'd just run five miles. Her lips were swollen and damp, and I fucking ached to have them wrapped around my cock.

"You don't go anywhere without me," I told her in a voice thick with all the hunger gnawing at my insides. "I ever see another guy that close to you, and I'll put a bullet in his head. Understand?"

"I didn't do anything wrong," she snapped, that dazed and dreamy look in her eyes darkening to anger. "You act like I was cheating on you or something. Even if I was all over that guy, there's not a damn thing you can say about it. We aren't together, Theo."

"No?" I asked in a deceptively low voice, my own anger rising.

"No, we are not. I'm not your woman, or anything else that possessive, overly aggressive, alpha inner beast of yours seems to think. You don't own me. If anything, we're just friends. You'd made that clear as day until you pulled that shit at the club, growling at AJ like some Neanderthal." She made a grunting noise in the back of her throat that was sexy as fuck. "Mm. My woman. Mm. No touch."

Despite how pissed I was, I couldn't help tossing back my head and laughing at her imitation. Fuck, but she was adorable.

A ghost of a grin teased at her lips before she pouted out her kiss-swollen bottom lip and crossed her arms over her chest. "I'm being serious, Theo. You had no right to hit AJ."

"Stop fucking saying his name." I moved so fast, she squealed in surprise when I grabbed her legs and dragged her down the bed. I then straddled her legs, locking her in place without putting my full weight on her. "Deny it if it makes you feel better, Tavia. Punish me all you want by insisting you don't belong to me, but we both know the truth. You are mine. You have been from the first day I set eyes on you downstairs in the library. From that day on, I saw no one, wanted no one else but you. For three fucking years, I sat back and waited for you to finish growing up so I could claim what is rightfully mine."

"Wh-what?" she breathed, her eyes widening in wonder. "Y-you did?"

"From the day I saw you, krasotka. You claimed me—and my heart. I know I haven't shown you that, and I'm so damn sorry. I got so used to holding myself back over the years in order to protect you that I didn't know how to stop." Cupping the side of her face, I stroked my thumb over her baby-soft skin. "I love you, baby. I love you so goddamn much, but it has never scared me. The only thing I fear in this world is losing you."

Tears filled her eyes and quickly spilled over. Seeing them was like acid poured directly onto my heart, and I kissed them away. "Don't cry. Please, krasotka. I will do anything to stop your tears. Don't cry, because I love you. I can't stand it."

"I...I'm sorry," she whispered emotionally. "I'm just... It's hard to stop the tears when I never thought I would ever be this happy."

Relief that maybe I was finally doing something right where she was concerned washed over me. "Really?"

"I think I fell for you that first day, too," she confessed, her tears falling even faster now. "You walked into the room, and I couldn't make myself look away. I tried—hard. But no matter how many times I told myself I was acting like a stupid little girl with a crush, I couldn't not look at you. Because when I did, I felt this weird peace fill me, and I hadn't ever experienced that before."

A few strands of hair had fallen from her topknot, and I pushed them back from her face as I looked down at her. "Tell me you love me."

"I-I love you, Theo. I always have. Even when I hated you, I loved you." Her chin trembled.

"Please... Please don't break my heart, though. I-I really don't think I could survive that again."

"Ah, baby. I'm sorry. So fucking sorry. I won't ever hurt you again." Pressing my forehead to hers, I breathed in deeply. "I swear I didn't mean to make your heart hurt. When we made love that first night, I was a weak man. I knew better than to touch you before I could give you everything you deserved, but I couldn't resist. I left you the next morning because I didn't want Petrov to find out about us and use you against me. All I wanted was to protect you from the darkness for a little while longer."

"So you really didn't know I was his daughter?"

Lifting my head, I met her gaze. "You were his best-kept secret."

"But...why did you hate him so much?" she murmured, a frown pinching her brows together.

Grimacing, I moved so I was lying on my side and pulled her head onto my shoulder. "You know I'm adopted?" She nodded. "Pops is my uncle, but his name is actually on my birth certificate. My real dad, his brother, died while Pops was in prison. Petrov gave the order to take him out. As soon as I knew who was behind his death, I started plotting my revenge."

"I'm so sorry," she told me in a shaky voice. "I don't know how you don't hate me, too. I mean, I'm his daughter. I—"

I hushed her with a kiss, stopping the ugly words from touching either of our hearts. When I felt the tension ease from her shoulders, I lifted my head. "Nothing, ever, could make me hate you, Tavia. You are all that is good in this world. I don't know how you came from a man who was so evil, but by some miracle, you did. And for that, I'll always be thankful to the man."

"Does it make me a bad person that I'm glad you killed him and Yerik?" she asked hesitantly.

"No, baby. Not even a little," I assured her. "If anything, I would think it bad if you weren't at least a little glad Yerik is dead."

"He always made me feel uncomfortable. Maybe I should have just told your mom I didn't want him to drive me. But she was only being nice, and I didn't want to be rude." Her chin started trembling again. "If you hadn't shot him, he would have raped me. I know he would have."

Renewed rage at the motherfucker had my muscles twisting into knots. "No, he wouldn't have. Because I would have broken his fucking neck before I let him touch you again."

"I believe you."

TWENTY-THREE

Hearing those words coming from her was the best thing I'd ever heard outside of her saying she loved me. I couldn't hold back another second. I needed her, all of her.

"Did the doctor say anything about sex?" I rasped, kissing my way down her neck.

"He might have," she murmured.

"Tavia," I growled and was rewarded with her giggle.

"Yes, Theo. It's safe for us to have sex. It has been for over a week now. Maybe longer since I didn't really bleed much with the…" She trailed off, and when I looked at her face, it was to find fresh tears in her eyes. But I knew those weren't happy tears.

"With the miscarriage," she finished with a small sob.

All thoughts of my aching cock disappeared, and I sat up, taking her with me. But instead of begging her not to cry, this time, I urged her to go ahead. She needed to cry. Needed to let go and just grieve.

I'd been so worried about her the past few weeks because she'd never once spoken about the baby, but tonight I realized that was probably my fault as well since I never talked about it either. My only excuse wasn't a good enough one. That it hurt too much to think about what could have been.

We could have been a family. I could have had a son or daughter that was half the woman I loved more than life itself. I could have spoiled him or her, given them the best life a child could ever hope for. I could have tucked them into bed, read them stories like my parents had done for me, and loved them for eternity.

But by hiding from my pain, I'd made Tavia think it was okay to hide hers as well. I'd let her bottle it all up, suffer in silence, maybe even made her think I didn't care at all about the loss of the child we'd created out of the love we shared.

My own tears spilled over as I cupped the back of her head and cradled her against my chest. "It's okay, krasotka. Cry it all out. Grieve, my love." My voice cracked, and she wrapped her arms around me tightly, offering me comfort as I was her.

"All…" Another sob took her breath away, and she gasped, shaking her head against me. "All I can think is that I finally had someone who would have loved me. Who would have been all mine, and we could have been a family. I would have belonged to someone. And now that's… It's all gone, Theo. It was snatched away before I could even hold our baby."

"Tavia, you already belong to someone—me. And maybe you haven't realized it yet, but you already have a family. Raven and Felicity and Lexa. Mom and Pops and Sofia. You belong to all of us. We all love you. Completely. Unconditionally. Forever." After stroking a hand down her spine, I slid it around to her lower abdomen and touched the place where I imagined our child might have grown inside her. "I'm so sorry we lost our baby. But please don't think it was your only chance at having what you've always wanted. Because you already had it, long before I put that precious gift here."

One of her hands covered mine, pressing it closer. "I would have loved that baby with everything I am, Theo."

"Me too, krasotka. I loved our baby as soon as the doctor told me you were pregnant. And then with his next breath, he informed me you'd had a miscarriage. I felt like the world had shifted under my feet. It was as if I'd lost something vital without even realizing I needed it." I kissed her lips. It was just a soft brush of my lips over hers, not meant to be full of passion or to go anywhere, but because I couldn't not kiss her, not touch her, not show her how much she meant to me. "One day... One day, we will have another child. Maybe many. And we will show each of them how much we love them. But we will never forget this one. I promise you."

"More babies?" she murmured in wonder. "Y-you want to have more children with me?"

"I want to spend the rest of my life with you. If you bless me with more children, I would be overjoyed." I saw the indecision in her dark eyes and quickly amended, "But if you don't want to have children, that's okay too. All I want is you, Tavia. Everything else is just a bonus."

"Wh-what if I can't have more babies?" she asked in a voice loaded with pain and uncertainty.

"My sister and I were both adopted by amazing people. I wouldn't mind if we needed to go that route. Or if that is something you want to do just for the hell of it, I'm okay with it." I kissed her again, slower, pouring every ounce of my love for her into each caress of my lips against hers. "All I want is your happiness."

"All I want is you," she whispered, and then she was the one kissing me.

Tavia straddled my lap, her fingers stabbing into my hair, demanding I kiss her harder, deeper. I could feel her heat through our layers of clothes, the fine tremors in her body telling me how much she wanted me.

Hungrily, I tore at the material separating our bodies, needing to feel all of her against me. Needing more than anything to be inside her.

"Theo," she cried out when I thrust up into her hot tightness.

Finally being in the one place I never wanted to leave, I lost all control. I tightened my fingers on her perfect, amazing ass and held her in place as I thrust up into her until she was screaming for more. I felt her inner walls contracting around my cock, sending me closer to the edge of my own release.

"I love you, krasotka," I growled into her neck. "I love you so fucking much, baby."

"I-I love you too," she panted. "So much."

At those first three words, I lost the war on trying to hold back, and my cock started spurting my release deep into her body. Her body still shaking from her orgasm, Tavia fell against me, her slight weight pressing me back against the headboard as she gasped for breath, her fingernails scratching up and down my back unconsciously.

"Love you," she slurred sleepily, her breathing evening out and deepening.

I kissed her shoulder. "I love you, krasotka."

TWENTY-FOUR

Slowly, consciousness came back to me. The room was dim, the only light filtering in coming through the small crack left from where the drapes weren't completely closed. The warmth I felt was bordering on sweltering, and I lifted my head to find Theo plastered to my side, one of his legs wrapped over both of mine. One of his arms was over my back, while the other was under me, his chest and shoulder acting as my pillow.

When I shifted, he stirred. "Sleep, krasotka," he grumbled, still half asleep. "Let's stay in bed all day."

I felt my lips twitch in the beginnings of a smile, and I returned my head to his chest. "Okay," I agreed drowsily.

I felt him smile as he kissed the top of my head. "That's my girl."

Closing my eyes, I drifted back to sleep, content in the feel of his arms around me. It didn't matter that I was sweating from all his body heat or that I was basically tied to the bed with his limbs wrapped around me.

For the first time in maybe ever, I was happy. Truly, completely happy.

The next time I opened my eyes, it was to the sound of a tap on the bedroom door. Theo was no longer wrapped around me, and when I looked around the room, there was no sign he was there. Frowning because I thought he was going to stay in bed with me all day, I sat up just as the door opened and Mrs. Volkov walked into the room carrying a tray.

She beamed at me and didn't even blink when I hastily grabbed the covers and tucked them under my arms to hide my naked body from her. "I was going to let you sleep, but Theo called down to the kitchen earlier for a tray for the two of you, and then he got an urgent call to take care of something he didn't have time to explain to me. So, I thought I would bring up your lunch."

Wiping a hand over my face, I tried to focus on what she was saying. "Urgent?"

"I think it was more to do with your business holdings. He seemed out of humor when he ran out of here a little while ago." She placed the tray over my lap and straightened. "You look so much better today. I see your night out with Sofia did you some good. Although, I'm sure Sofia wouldn't agree with you. She went to school this morning with a major hangover."

I blinked at her, surprised she was so calm about her daughter having a hangover. "Um, yeah," I finally mumbled and picked up the spoon to take a bite of the Greek yogurt with fresh berries.

Her light laugh pulled my gaze back to her. "I remember sneaking out of my father's house with my sister so often, I can't exactly get mad at Sofia for doing the same. I can't tell you how many times I came home completely trashed, and Scarlett would have to put me to bed and make sure my glucose levels were within range before going to sleep herself. Sofia isn't nearly as wild as I was, so I have to be thankful for that much at least."

She turned to leave after giving me another kind smile. "When you're done, just leave the tray. Someone will fetch it."

I dropped the spoon back in the dish. "Mrs. Volkov?"

She turned at the door. "I really wish you would call me Victoria," she told me for what was probably the tenth time. "Or...maybe even Mom?"

My heart twisted at that hesitant suggestion, as if she were afraid I would turn her down. "R-really?" I whispered, my heart blooming with the love and respect I had for this woman.

She walked back to me, her eyes sad and a little hopeful. "I would sincerely love for you to call me Mom. And if Theo ever gets his head out of his ass, you will be my daughter one day. So, let's just cut out the middle ground of waiting for that day, and you start calling me 'Mom' now. Yeah?"

"I..." I cleared my throat, trying to get rid of the lump that was suddenly choking me. "Okay."

She sat on the edge of the bed, her eyes skimming over my face and making me blush. "What did you want to ask me?"

"It wasn't so much something I wanted to ask you, but tell you... Thank you. For everything you've done for me the last few weeks. It means a lot to me."

Grasping my hand, she gave it a gentle squeeze. "Anything for you, sweetheart." Her knowing brown eyes met mine. "I know things haven't been easy for you lately. Losing a child is not something I've ever had to face personally, but I do know what it's like to have my heart feel like it has been shattered into a billion pieces. So, if you need anything, even if it's just a shoulder to cry on or someone to vent to, I'm here for you. Always."

"Th-thank you," I whispered.

After she left, I slowly finished the meal she'd brought. The yogurt was accompanied by a sandwich and a light salad, along with fruit juice and a cup of coffee. I ate it all, surprising myself at how hungry I was, then placed the tray at the foot of the bed before going into the bathroom to shower.

Since Theo was gone, I took my time, enjoying the feel of the spray on my muscles. When I walked back into the bedroom a long while later, it was to find Theo standing by the window, his arms crossed over his chest as he glared out at the late afternoon sky.

"What's wrong?" I asked, already starting to worry about whatever had put that fierce look on his face.

Turning his head, Theo skimmed his gaze over me from head to toe and back again, appreciation in his dark eyes. Seeing me seemed to relax him a little, and he unfolded his arms, spreading them wide and silently beckoning me.

Without hesitation, I walked into his outstretched arms and wrapped my own around his waist. "What's wrong?" I repeated.

"Just work stuff, baby," he murmured, kissing a trail down my neck, causing me to shiver deliciously. "You have more businesses than I anticipated, and the changeover isn't going as smoothly as I would like. But I've sorted it out." His teeth nipped at my shoulder. "I'm sorry I wasn't here when you woke. I wanted to stay in bed and make love to you all day."

I didn't even care about all the businesses and money he and his dad said I had inherited. If he wanted to deal with them, I wasn't going to stop them, but in all honesty, I wanted nothing to do with them.

"I'm not opposed to you doing that all night," I said with a coy little smile as I looked up at him through my lashes.

His groan sounded like it was being torn from him. "Fuck, I want nothing more than that. But I have a request."

"Anything."

"Let's go to my apartment. It's in the city and closer to your university. I would like to make that our home until we find a house—if you want a house. The apartment is two floors. I combined the one I stayed in before Mom and Pops married and Pops's personal apartment into my own space." He stroked both his hands down my back, distracting me. "There would be plenty of space for babies."

Butterflies fluttered in my stomach at the way he said "babies," and I melted against him. "Sounds perfect," I assured him. "But why the sudden move?"

He sighed. "Because I want to make love to you day and night without having to worry if my mom is going to walk in at any moment. Or if Sofia will barge in without knocking. I want to fuck you in the living room, and bent over the kitchen table, or up against the wall outside the elevator. But there are way too many people running around this house for me to do any of those things."

I pressed my thighs together, trying to relieve the throb deep between my legs as my mind filled with all kinds of decadent images of us fulfilling all of those fantasies. "Okay. Then let's get me moved in."

His entire body seemed to relax. "Yeah?"

I nodded, grinning up at him. "If we hurry, you might get the chance to fuck me in all those places before the end of the night."

Epilogue

THREE YEARS LATER

Nervously, I sat in the back of the limo, waiting for the jet to taxi over to this side of the private airport.

I hadn't seen Raven since the previous Thanksgiving when Theo had surprised me with a trip to Northern California to visit the people whom I had lovingly come to think of as my extended family. In the past three years, we'd gone to visit at least two or three times a year, but this was the first time Raven was coming to me.

With the summer vacation having just started, Nova and Garret were coming for their usual weeks-long visit, but Raven and her husband were also joining Flick and Jet this time to attend our wedding. Something I was still having a hard time believing was actually happening.

Over the previous Christmas, Theo had taken me to St. Petersburg, and it had been one of the most beautiful places I'd ever seen. The snow on the ground, the lights, all the amazing architecture. And to see it at night... It was dream I didn't know I had come true.

And there, with the colorful lights glittering off the snow, Theo had proposed to me.

I got butterflies in my stomach just remembering the tears in his eyes as he'd asked me to be his wife. How I'd whispered "yes" a hundred times, my own tears streaming down my face until he kissed me quiet. It was a moment in time I was never going to forget.

As soon as we'd gotten home, his mom and aunts had been ready to start the wedding preparations, and I'd gotten lost in the fun of dress shopping, cake tasting, venue hunting with the woman I now called Mom as easily as I called Theo mine. But she would be sitting on Theo's side on our wedding day, and I felt like I had no one to sit on mine.

Until Raven accepted the wedding invitation I sent her. She and Flick had promised me there was nothing that could stop them from showing up and being my family. And that was all I needed. The two of them were more than enough, and I couldn't help loving them even more for doing something so special for me.

Finally, the Vitucci private jet stopped about fifty yards away, and the door opened. Someone stepped out, and I watched as Nova skipped down the stairs. The back door of the limo in front of the one I was sitting in opened, and Ryan got out. Seeing him, Nova took off at full speed and launched herself at the teenager like a rocket, laughing so happily that the sound made me smile.

Theo chuckled and shook his head as he watched the same scene I was. "That never gets old."

"Yeah," I murmured. "I love seeing them reunite."

Turning his gaze on me, he lifted his hand to stroke his thumb down my cheek. "Ready for this?"

I nodded. "I don't know why I'm so nervous. I speak to her on the phone at least once a week. It's not like we don't know what's going on in each other's lives at any given time."

"Because she's important to you, that's why. And you're excited to see her." Entwining his fingers with mine, he gave a little tug and opened the door. "Come on. Let's go greet them."

When we stepped out, there were four goons in suits standing by the first limo. But once Ryan had Nova inside, the goons climbed into the limo, and it drove off. Without Nova's parents or her brother, who were all now coming down the stairs.

"Not even a 'See you later, Daddy' or an 'I love you, Daddy,'" Jet grumbled as he glared after the limo. "You would think I don't even exist."

"When Ryan's around, no one exists to Nova," Flick told him with a grin. "You already knew that, babe."

"Yeah, yeah," he said with a grunt.

Reaching the bottom of the stairs, Flick hugged me. "It's so good to see you, sweetheart," she murmured.

"I'm so glad you could all make it," I told her, hugging her back, then accepting one from Jet, who kissed my cheek.

"I want hugs too," a voice I wasn't expecting called down.

Looking up, I saw both Monroe and Mila bouncing down the stairs, followed by their brother and parents. Mila's hair was still dyed darker than her twin's, but her makeup wasn't nearly as emo punk rocker as it had once been. In the past few years, I'd noticed the slow change in her style, and I had to say I liked it.

My heart clenched as, one by one, I watched all of the Hannigan men and their wives and children exit behind the Mastersons. Hawk, Colt, and Raider had all become surrogate uncles to me just as Raven said they would, and in the past three years, I'd come to love them all.

Tears choked me as Raven finally appeared at the door and waved down at me. "Hey, kiddo!" she yelled. "Save me some love, would ya?"

I was already being hugged to within an inch of my life by the thickly muscled, burly blond men I called uncles. But as soon as she was in front of me, I was hugging her for all I was worth. "I thought it was only going to be you and Flick," I half sobbed.

"Couldn't let your side of the church be empty, now could I?" she murmured. Pulling back, she shook her head at me. "Why you crying, girl? You're not supposed to start the waterworks until tomorrow when you walk down the aisle."

"I'm just so happy to see you," I told her, trying to stop the flow of tears.

"Lexa wanted to come," she said with a twist of her lips. "But the doctor wouldn't let her fly since she's so close to her due date. Which means, unfortunately, I have to head back tomorrow night after the wedding in case she goes into labor early."

"I understand," I promised her. "I'm just thankful you could come at all."

"I wouldn't have missed this for anything."

As we were talking, several black SUVs pulled up behind us, and I realized Theo must have known that more than just Flick and Raven were coming. When I glanced at him and he winked, I threw my arms around him, kissing him until I was out of breath. "Thank you," I whispered, fighting back the lump in my throat.

"Anything to make you happy, krasotka."

NEXT FROM
TERRI ANNE BROWNING

Savoring Mila

**Angels Halo MC Next Gen &
Rockers' Legacy Series (Crossover)**

Book 3

Loving Violet

Rockers' Legacy Series

Book 4

Surviving His Scars

Angels Halo MC Series

Book 4

CPSIA information can be obtained
at www.ICGtesting.com
Printed in the USA
BVHW030249190421
605284BV00015B/409

CPSIA information can be obtained
at www.ICGtesting.com
Printed in the USA
LVHW040823200723
752995LV00003B/40